by
MARY AMATO

illustrations and sketches by
ANTONIO CAPARO

EGMONT
USA

New York

EGMONT

We bring stories to life

First published by Egmont USA, 2009
443 Park Avenue South, Suite 806
New York, NY 10016

Text copyright © Mary Amato, 2009
Illustrations copyright © Antonio Caparo, 2009
All rights reserved

1 3 5 7 9 8 6 4 2

www.egmontusa.com
www.maryamato.com

Library of Congress Cataloging-in-Publication Data

Amato, Mary.
Invisible lines / by Mary Amato ; illustrations by Antonio Caparo.
p. cm.
Summary: Coming from a poor, single-parent family, seventh-grader Trevor must rely
on his intelligence, artistic ability, quick wit, and soccer prowess to win friends at his
new Washington, D.C. school, but popular and rich Xander seems determined to cause
him trouble.
ISBN 978-1-60684-010-8 (hardcover) — ISBN 978-1-60684-043-6 (reinforced library
binding) [1. Social classes—Fiction. 2. Middle schools—Fiction. 3. Schools—Fiction.
4. Single-parent families—Fiction. 5. Moving, Household—Fiction. 6. Washington,
D.C.—Fiction.] I. Caparó, Antonio, ill. II. Title.
PZ7.A49165Inv 2009
[Fic]—dc22
2009014639

Printed in the United States of America

For the Trevors I have known.

—*M.A.*

CONTENTS

1.
MUSGROVE

If there's one thing I'm good at it's making people laugh because when I'm standing up I'm what you call a stand-up comedian, and when I'm sitting down, I'm just plain funny.

We're sitting on the bus. I'm on one side, sandwiched between two big women, and Michael and Mom are on the other side with Tish on Mom's lap. Michael and Tish are whining, which means my mom is ready to explode, so I suck in my cheeks and bug out my eyes like I'm a hot dog being squished to death by the bun and they all laugh.

The bus stops, and I whip out my fine point and draw a squished hot dog on Michael's arm so he can keep looking at it.

"Me!" Tish says, and holds out her arm.

"Stop doing that, Trevor," Mom says. "That ink is gonna sink in like poison."

But she knows Tish will have a fit if I don't do one on her, so I give her a quick little hot-dog tattoo, and Tish grins.

We're still not there.

The bus rumbles over a pothole, and everybody settles back into being quiet. Mom gets tense and sad again, but I'm not because I have decided that it's going to be my year. The year of Trevor Musgrove.

When the bus stops again, I draw my name graffiti-style on my shoe. Michael takes his thumb out of his mouth and asks, "What does it say?"

"It's our last name. Musgrove."

"How come you're writing it on your shoe?"

"What?" My mom snaps into focus. "Don't scribble all over them shoes, Trev."

Tish takes her eyes off her new tattoo to see what we're talking about.

I pretend I don't hear her because I'm not scribbling. It's a masterpiece. I wave some air over it.

"You drying it?" Michael asks.

Musgrove. It's going to be my year.

I do the other shoe by the time the bus pulls
over, and Mom says, "This is it."

Lights are flashing in the parking lot—
four police cars, one ambulance—and a crowd is
gathered around some Dumpsters that are blocked
off with yellow tape.

It takes us a while to get off the bus because
I've got three garbage bags, and Mom has a big
box, which means she can't carry Tish. The driver
is leaning over the wheel, head on his arms, eyes
closed, like he's ready to lie down and die.

Finally we make it out, and Michael takes his
thumb out of his mouth.

"Why's they here?" he asks, looking at the
police.

"It's a welcome parade 'cause we're moving in,"
I say, and my mom laughs.

"Come on. We're over here," she says, and starts
leading the way.

Tish pulls on my shorts. "Me up."

"Me can't," I say. "See me hands? Me hands full. Come on, Little Cavewoman."

I call Michael "Little Man" because he's so serious, and then I started calling Tish "Little Cavewoman" because she talks like one, which I think is cute. She'd probably hate it if she were older, but she doesn't even know what a cave-woman is.

We pass a sign for the complex: HEDLEY GARDENS APARTMENTS. Somebody has scratched out *Hedley* and written the word *Deadly* above it. Mom steers us clear of the Dumpsters, even though Michael keeps asking what's going on, because she doesn't want us to hear about any-thing bad. But then a skinny girl who looks about my age says, like she's the mayor of the city and it's her job to fill us in, "They found a baby in the Dumpster." She says it loud and clear, like she's got a microphone. "A real baby somebody threw out. It's a he, but he don't have a name."

My mom hustles us on, but another guy who is walking up asks the skinny girl what's going on.

"High school girl had a baby and threw it in the Dumpster."

"Man, she should've let it be adopted," he says. "Rich people pay ten thousand bucks for a baby."

"Maybe her daddy would kill her if he knew she was having it."

I want to find out if the baby is okay, but Mom is speed-walking.

"This one is our building! Hold on! Be careful, Tish! Trev, watch Tish!" she says because there's broken glass on the steps, and her voice is sounding funny like it's about to break, too. "We have to walk up," she says.

No elevator. No surprise.

It's okay. Every time I take a step, I see the new *Musgrove*s on my shoes. Looks like they came from the store that way, all professional, if I do say so myself.

"Floor number five," she says.

"That's me," Michael says. "I'm five."

"You're right!" Mom says. "You're my big kindergartner. Doing a good job with that backpack, too." She's using her fake happy voice.

"Me five," Tish says.

"You is not. You's two," Michael yells.

Tish stands still and glares at Michael with her

perfectly round little face all fierce. "Me five!"

She cracks me up. "Keep your pants on, Little Cavewoman," I say. "You're five in your mind, right?"

"Me five." She nods.

"You is not," Michael says, and I promise to play Superheroes with him later so he'll shut up. Then I have to watch Tish because she wants to pick up every piece of trash along the way.

"Yuck." I grab each thing out of her hands, except for a piece of blue chalk that she buries in her fist.

"Looks like somebody else likes to scribble on everything," Mom says. "Don't you go getting any ideas, Trev."

She's ahead of me, so it isn't until I turn on to the next floor that I see the graffiti. Just F-words and random lines and skulls. *That's* scribble.

Number 513. Mom unlocks the door. Two rooms: tiny and dirty and empty and hot. Hole punched in one wall that nobody bothered to fix.

Michael takes his thumb out of his mouth and plugs his nose. "How come it stinks in here?"

"Look! A nice big window! Why don't you open

it and get some fresh air in, Trev."

I open the window. "Guess what we got a view of?"

"What?" Michael asks.

"Don't matter," Mom says. "Come here and help me get this stuff out, Michael." She opens a garbage bag and pulls out the orange shoe box with our photos and important papers in it.

She doesn't want him to see the Dumpster crowd because he'll ask what's going on again. Ambulance guys wearing bright blue gloves are carrying an orange shoe box to the ambulance.

"Hey, Mom. They've got the same shoe box."

"Shut up, Trev," she says. "I don't want to hear about it."

I can tell by the way they're holding the shoe box that the baby is inside and still alive.

Michael takes his thumb out. "Can we go home now? I don't like this place."

It's like that old-time story about the little kid who blurts out what everybody else is thinking. The emperor has no clothes! Except in this case it's: This place is trash.

Mom doesn't want to hear it. She sits on the

floor and pulls Michael to her. "Baby, this is home now. We're living here." She kisses him, and Tish squeezes in for a kiss, too.

People start yelling at each other in the apartment directly below ours. Michael stares at the floor as if at any minute their voices are going to explode through it. Outside, the siren of the ambulance begins to wail.

My mom's eyes fill up with water and she holds herself real still like somebody put her on the edge of a cliff and she's afraid she'll fall if she moves. She does this when she's upset. She turns herself into a statue and she doesn't blink because she doesn't like to cry.

"You know what we need to do?" I say. "We need to do us a little decorating. We need a picture on the wall." I pick up the stick of blue chalk that Tish found.

"Make a tree picture," Michael says.

I've always been especially good at drawing trees.

Mom gives me this "don't you dare" look, but I start to draw on the wall.

"Trev, you can't do that—" she says, but she's too tired to stop me and we both know it'll wash off.

"Ta-da!"

Mom starts laughing.

Little Cavewoman waddles over, takes the chalk, and starts scribbling on the wall.

"No, Tish!" Mom jumps up, still laughing, and she wipes her eyes real fast and takes the chalk

away. "That was a joke. It's called laughing just to keep from crying. We got to wash it off, baby. We don't draw on walls. See what you taught her, Trev?"

"I don't want to wash it off," Michael says, but Mom is already digging in the box for a sponge.

Outside, the crowd is almost gone. There's only one police car left. It bothers me that the baby doesn't have a name. Everybody should have a name.

Michael walks over and leans on the windowsill, sucking his thumb.

"Let's think up a name for that little baby," I whisper.

He pops his thumb out of his mouth and whispers back, "Charlie."

Charlie it is.

With the blue chalk I write CHARLIE on the inside of the windowsill, where Mom won't see it. "Shh, don't tell," I whisper to Michael.

"What does it say?"

"Charlie."

"Why you writing it?"

"Putting a name down is important. It makes a person official. Charlie."

"Put my name down," Michael says.

"If you stop sucking your thumb."

Michael's thinking about it.

I write Tish's name. And Mom's. And mine.

Michael takes his thumb out of his mouth.

I write his name.

"Now we're all imported," he says.

"Important. Not imported. We want to be important."

"Yeah," he says. And then he sticks his thumb back in his mouth.

2.
KA-CHING

Bam. School starts. It's weird because even though Deadly Gardens is a giant step down, this school is definitely a step up. It's in the rich-looking neighborhood on the other side of Branch Road. Buckingham School. Clean and spiffy. Gleaming blue lockers. The locker number assigned to me is number 333. Straight-up lucky number.

I've got it written on a yellow card, and I'm trying to find the three hundreds when I see the Manchester United guys. They have on Manchester United jerseys—the real deals, not fakes—and new Nike shoes. They look like they jumped out of a soccer catalog. One is real strong and tall and has light brown hair cut short. He's holding up his cell phone and a little crowd is watching some kind of video on it. The other one looks fast and loose. He's got long wavy red hair in a ponytail that could look stupid, but he pulls it off. Everybody cheers at something on the phone, and then the red-haired one acts out this routine where he's getting hit in the head slo-mo style and everybody's laughing.

Juan, this quiet guy who was on my bus, is walking by, so I ask him who the guys are.

The tall guy is Xander Pierce, and the one with the long hair is Langley McCloud, he tells me. Xander is short for Alexander, which is too cool. Wish I had a name like that. "They're in the Summit," Juan adds. I want to know what that means, but he has already walked on.

I'm planning on getting a look at what's on the phone and slipping Xander one of my funny comments to score a solid first impression when that skinny loudmouthed girl—the one from

Deadly Gardens who broadcast the news about the Dumpster baby—comes walking down the hall with a friend, singing like she's the next American Idol. *"If you love me, baby, set me free!"*

Xander groans and calls out, "It's too early for torture."

"That's why I'm not looking at your face," the girl says back.

Langley laughs.

Xander gets in another one right away. "Looks like the janitor forgot to pick up the trash again."

"When I'm famous, you're gonna regret you said that," she says, "'cause you ain't getting my autograph."

He's saying something back, but she recognizes me and steers her friend over like she's coming to talk to me. Last thing I need is to be identified with her. I turn my back and glue myself to locker number 218, even though it isn't mine, and start working the lock in the hopes that she'll see I'm busy and leave me alone.

"Hey," she says. Her voice is as loud as a truck. "How come you didn't say hi to me on the bus?

This is my partner, Celine. I'm Diamond. We're gonna be a famous female recording duo."

"Stop telling everybody that!" Celine laughs and hits Diamond. "I'm gonna chicken out."

"You can't chicken out," she says to Celine. Then she turns to me. "We're signing up to audition for the talent show." She leans back and lets it rip. *"If you love me, baby, set me free!"*

I pretend like I don't hear her, which would be a major miracle if it were true, because it's like this girl swallowed a microphone at birth and the batteries are still working. Xander and Langley have walked away, which is good.

"You having trouble with that?" Diamond asks.

I'm thinking about throwing out some signs like I'm deaf, but that would be hard to pull off. "Nah. I'm cool," I say.

"Oooooh, he's cool," Celine says.

A skinny kid who looks like a mosquito zooms in from out of nowhere and says, "Um. I think that's my locker." He sticks his yellow card with the locker number in my face.

Diamond whips my yellow card right out of my

hand and reads it. "You're 333. I'm 327. It's right up here." She pulls my arm and starts singing. *"If you love me, baby, set me free!"*

Mosquito Boy calls after me. "Um. How could you possibly think 218 was 333?"

First two minutes of school and I'm stuck between Mosquito and Microphone Mouth. Not a good sign.

"Here you go," Diamond says, and flashes me a hero smile, like if it wasn't for her I'd be trying to find locker number 333 for the rest of my life.

"Oooh," Celine says. "You're neighbors."

Diamond laughs, and Celine pulls her away.

Locker number 333. Straight-up *un*lucky number. Why couldn't I be neighbors with Xander and Langley?

It's stupid but my heart is going *bam bam bam* while I'm dialing up the combination. I always wanted a locker, but my old school didn't have them, so I'm not sure if I'm doing it right.

I turn the lock too far past the last number of the combination and have to start again. *Focus. Focus. Focus.*

Ka-ching! It opens!

The skinny blankness of it is just plain beautiful. My locker. My space.

Have to do it again. *Ka-ching!* Feels so good when it swings open.

I'm dying to write my name on the door. Just small on the inside to make the locker really mine. *Trevor Musgrove.* Wish I had a cool name like Xander Pierce. I could do a lot with that.

"Eh-eh-eh—" A passing teacher grabs the fine point out of my hand. "We do not deface school property."

"That's my only good marker," I call out.

"It's mine now," the teacher says without turning back.

"I promise I won't write on it. Please—"

Down the hall, Diamond saw the whole thing and now she's laughing.

I borrow a piece of paper and take out a regular pen. Wish I had some thick plain paper and a new permanent fine point. I like quality. But as my mom says, you have to make do with what you got.

I write *Trevor Musgrove* on a scrap. Then ask around and nobody has tape so I run to the nearest room and successfully beg some off a teacher because I've got finesse. I'm almost late to class, but *almost* isn't late, and now my locker door is officially *Musgrove*d.

3.
MR. FUNGUS

I'm hoping all day that I'll be in a class with Xander and his buddy. But who do I have in almost every class so far? Microphone Mouth. At lunch I waste a lot of time in the line so that everybody else is sitting down, and then I choose the table with zip-lipped Juan, and I get the lay of the land, which is my strategy. First impressions stick like glue, my mom says. I need to scope things out before I make mine.

Xander and Langley's table definitely looks the best. The guys are playing table football with a folded-up piece of paper. There's a bunch of girls at the other end, all flirty.

Easy to notice the table where lots of kids from the Deadly Gardens bus are sitting, because Microphone Mouth is there . . . standing out. Seriously. She's standing at the table, dancing and singing her routine.

"Have a seat, Diamond!" the lunch lady says. They're on a first-name basis and I'm guessing it's *not* because they're friends.

The lunch lady can't see it, but Xander flicks the paper football at Diamond, and it hits her right in the back.

Xander's table cracks up.

Diamond turns around and throws a Tater Tot in their direction, and the lunch lady marches over and gives her a detention.

"Hey, Juan," I say. "What did you mean about those guys being in something called the Summit?"

"The Summit Program. It's like special classes you had to apply for," he explains. "The smart kids are in it. That's a Summit table." He nods at Xander and Langley's table.

There goes my chance of being in class with those guys.

I'm bored all day—except when I get lost three times, and then I'm humiliated—but when I get to my second-to-last class, Science Investigations, room 18, I'm stunned. Xander and Langley are sitting at one of the lab tables.

My jaw is still hitting the floor when the teacher says, "This is room 18. Summit Science Investigations. My name is Mr. Ferguson. If you are in the right place, find a seat quickly. If you are in the wrong place, find the exit quickly. We have a lot to accomplish in a short amount of time."

Right away my stomach gets a little sick because I know I'm in the wrong place. This is a Summit class. I check my schedule card twice. Room 18. Ferguson. Somebody made a mistake.

I should tell the teacher, but Xander is looking at me, so I pick the table next to theirs and sit down. Stools instead of chairs. And the stools all have tennis balls stuck on the bottom of each leg. I'm closest to Langley, so I lean over and ask him, "What's with the tennis balls?"

I'm playing it cool, but I'm prepared at any moment to hear the voice of God saying: "TREVOR MUSGROVE, YOU ARE GUILTY OF IMPERSONATING A SUMMIT STUDENT."

Langley looks down. "They keep the stools from squeaking." He jiggles back and forth on the seat to show how the tennis balls keep the feet from making noise.

I'm about to make a brilliantly funny comment when Mosquito Boy zooms in. "Um. Is anybody sitting here?" He takes the seat next to mine. "You're the one who got mixed up with my locker, right? You thought 218 was 333?"

Yeah, why don't you speak a little louder because I'm sure the whole class needs to hear how stupid I am.

"This place smells like a garbage dump," Xander whispers to Langley.

I was so amazed to see them when I walked in that I wasn't paying attention to the room. The lab tables are clean, but everything else is a mess. Buckets of dirt and sawdust all over. It does smell. But not garbagy. It reminds me of a pumpkin patch I went to on a field trip once. Plastic bags with something weird growing out of them are hanging from the ceiling. It's mushrooms. A whole lot of white mushrooms with real thin stems are growing from the plastic bags! This teacher must be seriously into mushrooms. There are mushroom posters everywhere. On his desk, which is actually a lab table that's raised up on a platform, he's got a mushroom paperweight and a mushroom cookie jar and even a pencil cup shaped like a mushroom.

Xander and Langley notice it at the same time. "What's with all the mushrooms?" Xander asks.

"Of all the things to be into . . . why would anybody pick that?" Langley whispers back.

I see my opportunity and go for it. Leaning over slightly I add, "Teacher even looks like a mushroom." He does. He's old and short with honey-brown skin and he's got a little white Afro.

They laugh.

Love the sound of that.

"Like an old dead *shiitake* mushroom," I add, and they laugh again.

Score.

Mr. Ferguson starts taking roll, calling each student's full name with a Mr. or Ms. in the front, and I start sweating. My name is not going to be on the list, and then everybody is going to know I'm Mr. Imposter.

"Mr. Anthony Barringer?"

"Here."

"Ms. Diana Chen?"

"Here."

By the time he gets to *M*, I'm so nervous I think I'm going to puke.

"Mr. Langley McCloud?"

"Here."

"Mr. Trevor Musgrove?"

I'm on his list! Hearing my name, plus the fact that it sounds all formal, is such a surprise, I blurt out "present" in my fake British accent.

Score more on the laugh-o-meter.

Mr. Ferguson puts down his pencil and looks over his glasses at me, like he's got X-ray vision and he's going to figure out in an instant what kind of joker he's got in his class.

Langley straightens up. He doesn't want to cross the line with Mr. Ferguson. My mom says everybody has an invisible line, so figure out where it is and don't cross it. Last year I crossed the line too much, but I want this year to be different, so I look Ferguson right back in the eye with my "I'll be good" face and then he says—completely deadpan—in *his* fake British accent, "Ah! Jolly good, Mr. Musgrove. Being present is more important than being here." Everybody laughs and he goes on with the roll.

I'm not sure how it happened, but I'm in.

When he finishes taking roll he stands, and I'm ready for the usual boring list of the same old rules and objectives and grading policies, but instead he picks up a wooden walking stick and a little brown cap like the kind Irish people wear in old movies. "How many of you noticed the precipitation late last night?"

A few people raise their hands.

"Lucky for us. Bring your Identification Notebooks and a writing utensil. We shall begin with a foray! A valuable prize goes to the first person to find a mushroom." He practically leaps to the door.

A foray?

Everybody is pulling out notebooks and pencils like they know what he's talking about. *Stay calm,* I tell myself. *Just watch everybody else and figure out what to do.* Langley pulls out this high-quality notebook with thick white pages, no lines. I love paper with no lines. Unfortunately, I don't have a notebook. I borrow a few sheets of paper from Mosquito Boy and take my best pen. We follow Ferguson into the bright hot sunshine toward a grassy and wooded area behind the school. He's all jaunty with his Irish cap on a tilt, walking fast and tapping his stick like a little old leprechaun, not even looking back to see if we're following.

"What a perfect day for a foray with utensils!" Langley whispers in his fake British accent, which cracks me up.

"Any day is a perfect day to get out of prison," I say.

If this were one of my other classes, everybody would be fooling around—Diamond, who is in almost all of my morning classes, got in trouble twice already, once in history for mouthing off and once in math for singing during class—but all these guys have their eyes to the ground, wanting to be the first to find a mushroom. Maybe that's what it means to be in the Summit Program.

It's nice back here behind the school. The grass is spongy and smells fresh. Maybe because of last night's *precipitation*, as Mr. Ferguson would say.

Eyes to the ground, Musgrove. It would be very cool if I could find a mushroom first. What's ironic here is that I hate mushrooms. Once when my mom and I had to stay in the shelter before Michael and Tish were even born, it rained all night and when I woke up I saw something sticking up along one wall . . . brown mushrooms with long thin stems right by my cot. That place gave me the creeps.

"My dad did a photo shoot of mushrooms for *National Geographic*," Xander says. "Sometimes they're on dead wood and sometimes in grass around trees or near a wet place. You just have to zone in. . . ."

I don't find anything but a dead leaf and a stick.

After a minute Xander bends down. "Bingo. Check it out."

"Hey, we found one," Langley calls out to the teacher.

Mr. Ferguson hustles over like we just found a golden goose egg. "We have a winner! Take a look!" He calls everybody over.

"What's our prize?" Langley asks.

"Hey, I'm the one who found it," Xander says.

Mr. Ferguson bows to Xander. "You have won my respect as well as your own satisfaction in a job well done. A valuable prize, indeed."

Xander bows back. Some of the girls clap and giggle.

Mr. Ferguson points at the mushroom in the grass with his walking stick. "Snow-white cap and stalk. Mr. Pierce, gently bend the mushroom so we can look under the cap. What do you see?"

"Pink ridges," Xander says.

"Those are gills. *Agaricus campestris*. Commonly called meadow mushroom or pink bottom."

Langley grins. "When my dad asks me what I did in science today, I get to say I saw a pink bottom."

Everybody laughs. Mr. Ferguson, too. Then the teacher asks if mushrooms belong in the plant kingdom or the animal kingdom. When everyone votes for plant, he gets a big kick out of it, pumping his stick on the ground. "Wrong. Wrong. Wrong."

"Wait! It's a fungus, right?" Xander blurts out.

"Ha! Another gold star for Mr. Pierce. The kingdom of fungi! A mushroom is a fungus!" He looks at us. Even though he's old, he's got these twinkling little-boy eyes and a spray of big brown freckles by his nose like maybe his mom sneezed pepper on him when he was born.

"The fungus among us," Langley says.

"Yes!" Mr. Ferguson laughs.

Wish I'd thought of that one.

"A fungus is neither plant nor animal," Mr. Ferguson goes on. "By the end of this unit, you will be fungal experts. Now, a scientist's most important feature is his or her—"

"Foot fungus," Langley whispers to me under his breath.

"—eyes." Mr. Ferguson points to his eyes.

"Take Leonardo da Vinci. Who was he?"

"An artist," a girl says.

"He was an artist, but he was also a scientist. Before photography was invented, scientists drew sketches to record observations and make identifications. Photography is a great thing, but it has made our powers of observation lazy. You cannot be lazy when you draw! Impossible! Why?"

"You have to pay attention to what you're drawing in order to draw it," Xander says.

"Yes! When you draw, you must look, and when you begin to look, you begin to see." He leans on his stick and looks from face to face, showing what it means to really look. His eyes are the deepest brown I've ever seen. Then he snaps out of it and waves his stick. "There are several other meadow mushrooms around. Get close to one. Draw, label, and date it in your Kingdom of Fungi Identification Notebooks. This will be entry number one. Any questions?"

While the others go off in search of more mushrooms, Xander, Langley, and I sit around this mushroom, and they begin to draw it. I draw a picture of Mr. Ferguson as a fungus and show it to the guys when the teacher's back is turned.

Langley laughs, and it cracks me up because he's got this funny laugh—it's kind of wavy like his hair. Of course, when Ferguson looks over, it's me he catches. "Is there something you'd like to share with the class, Mr. Musgrove?"

"No, sir."

I slip a blank sheet of paper over the drawing.

"I see you don't have an Identification Notebook," Mr. Ferguson says.

"I didn't know I needed one."

"You didn't receive the orientation packet?"

My stomach tightens. This is when he's going to find out that I'm in the wrong class. "I didn't know I was supposed to bring it on the first day."

He straightens up and talks to everyone. "A reminder. This notebook will be seventy-five percent of your first-quarter grade. In it you will keep your notes from class and from your reading as well as the entries. You'll be drawing, labeling, and discussing the properties of different types of fungi. Keep your eyes open. Once you start looking for mushrooms, you'll start seeing them in places you never noticed before. Sketch those, too. And—" He lifts one finger in the air. "This is important—I want to read your *thoughts* about what you're learning. Not just the facts. Facts I can get from a book."

I borrow another sheet and get to work on the mushroom.

Tap goes his stick by my foot. "Use your eyes," Mr. Ferguson says. "Draw what you see. And then you will see more." He taps his stick again. "If there is any reason why you cannot acquire a notebook, see me after class. Otherwise, I'll expect to see it tomorrow."

I forget about everything but the mushroom. I get up close and personal. I draw exactly what I see, every bump, every shadow.

"Discuss the properties of mushrooms?" Xander says under his breath. "How much can you say about a mushroom?"

Langley looks at my drawing. "Dude, that's ridiculous. You're definitely getting an A on that. Xander, check this out."

Langley asks what class I have next and when I say P.E., he looks glad and says, "Us, too."

I'm in.

AGARICUS CAMPESTRIS
(meadow mushroom)

← CAP

← GILLS
← ANNULUS
← STALK

This guy feels sturdy. Mr. Ferguson said that "toadstools" is an old nickname for mushrooms

Fungi are used to produce penicillin and other drugs that save lives.

4.
GOAL

"Okay, people, the first unit will be soccer," the P.E. teacher says, and I want to break into my victory dance because soccer is my sport. My mom says it's because I have some Brazilian blood in me. "By the way, tryouts for the school soccer team are two weeks from tomorrow. Just to warn you . . . it's a seventh-eighth-grade team, so there aren't many spots open to seventh graders."

I didn't know this was even possible. This is so cool. At my old school they only let eighth graders try out for teams, so I've never played on one.

Coach Stevins takes us outside—out of prison

twice in one day!—and goes over the rules for soccer. Ordinarily this would be boring, but he's funny to watch because he paces when he walks and has big shoulders and no neck.

I say to Langley and Xander, "Is it just me or does he look like a walking, talking refrigerator?"

They crack up.

The coach announces he's splitting us into mini teams for scrimmages.

"Whoever gets with Langley or Xander is going to fry everybody else," a girl says.

"I'm splitting them up," Coach Stevins says. Then he smiles. "Hey, I saw the catalog, Xander. Pretty darn cool."

Everybody looks at Xander in awe because none of us thought that refrigerators could smile.

"Yeah." Xander nods like it's no big deal. "I've done shoots before, but this was sweet because I got to keep all the gear."

"Stop by after class. You'll have to autograph my copy," Stevins says. "Okay people, let's get going."

When Stevins goes to get his clipboard, I do this

funny mock-bow to Xander and say, "I bow to the one who can maketh Coach Stevins lighten up."

He laughs.

I want to know what the catalog thing is about, but I can't ask because Stevins is back.

He divides us into six teams, making sure Xander and Langley are on different teams. I get on Langley's team, which is lucky. I won't be able to show Xander my skills because he's playing on a different team on the other side of the field, but I can show Langley what I've got. One thing's for sure. Everybody knows Xander and Langley are making the school team.

I jog over to where we're starting on the field, so excited I could spew.

Right before the game starts, some clouds swing in and cover the sun.

"Perfect way to play," Langley says.

I look up at the clouds. "Yeah, I ordered them on eBay."

He laughs.

"Hey, what was Stevins saying about Xander and some catalog?"

"Xander was on the cover of last month's Eurogear catalog."

I can't believe it. I thought Xander looked like somebody who stepped out of a catalog, and it turns out to be true.

Bam. Ball in. Game starts.

Langley is first to the ball. He passes it to me. Diamond is on the other team, and she gets right in my face, trying to distract me. *"You can't stop me now,"* she's singing, she's actually singing on the field.

I pull the ball back. "New strategy, huh? Sing in your opponent's face?"

"You can't stop me now!" she sings.

"Want to bet?" I sing back, do a smooth little fake, and leave her in the dust.

Diamond laughs.

I'm not worried about her. It's zip-lipped Juan, who is playing for the other team. He's real little, but he's unbelievably fast. Every time I get the ball, he's on me. I pass the ball to Langley, who tries to score twice. Finally we get one in. Langley does this funny victory jump.

The ball goes to their team. Juan fights off Langley, but Langley is determined to get it back. Juan passes it, Langley intercepts and pulls the ball away. He passes it to me, and I score before they know what hit them.

McCloud and Musgrove!

I let loose with my crazy victory dance, legs all wobbly, which makes everybody laugh.

Ball in again. Now Juan is on fire. He scores.

"Where did he come from?" Langley asks.

"Let's get it back," I say.

Now it's like Langley and I are connected by an invisible line and we can read each other's minds. I steal the ball, and Langley positions himself just right. My pass is high, but Langley jumps up and heads it in.

We get one more in before the whistle blows. Four to one.

I break into another victory dance. *McCloud and Musgrove!*

Sometimes life is so good it feels like you've got joy running inside your veins instead of blood.

On our way in, Langley and I walk together,

passing a ball back and forth, and he notices the *Musgrove* on my shoes and goes crazy when I tell him I did it myself. "What are you, like, a professional graphic designer?"

I tell him he'll be MVP for the school team and ask him how their season was last year.

"I don't know if we're trying out," he says. "Xander and I are on The Plague. It's an MCS Elite travel team. What league are you playing in?"

My mom says truth gets you respect and lies get you trouble, but sometimes I think you have to spruce up the truth a little to make the right impression. I can't tell him that I've never played anything but street soccer, so I tell him I haven't found a league yet because I just moved.

It works with Langley. "We're down a striker," he says. "You should try out. Tell your dad to check out the MCS Elite Web site or have him call my dad. He's one of the team managers. We're having the last tryout this Wednesday after school. Buckingham Park."

"Sure," I say, and nod like it's no big deal.

Inside I'm doing the craziest victory dance ever.

Xander joins up and starts in with a play-by-play of his game as we head back toward the school. I imagine that there's a movie camera above us, capturing this shot of three incredibly skilled soccer players talking and laughing and passing the ball back and forth as they walk down the field. *Pierce, McCloud, and Musgrove!*

"Hey," Langley says. "Musgrove is going to talk to his dad about trying out for The Plague."

Xander stops the ball. Unexpected silence.

"You should see him play," Langley says quickly. "We need another good striker."

I'm freaking out because it seems like Xander doesn't approve for some reason, but then Langley says, "Trust me. This guy can play."

Xander nods like it's cool and passes Langley the ball. I breathe a little sigh of relief.

"We missed first place last year because of a penalty kick in the last five minutes of the game," Xander explains to me. "It was a total crock. The ref was so biased. This year, we have to make first."

Langley passes me the ball and says to Xander,

"He's thinking about trying out for the school team, too. Right, Musgrove?"

"Yeah." I pass Xander the ball.

He stops it. "No. You don't want to do that. Coach Stevins doesn't know squat. He was a football player."

I look around. Lucky for Xander the coach isn't close enough to hear.

Langley shrugs. "I still think it might be fun."

"No way. We have to focus on taking The Plague to the top."

Langley pops up the ball and starts to dribble it. "The school team does have the worst name in the history of school names . . . the Toilets. Can you believe it?"

"No way."

"It's really the Toilers, but everybody says Toilets."

"You can't play for the Toilets," Xander adds. "It's just the dregs on that team. Besides, all the scouts come to check out the MCS Elite games."

Langley boots the ball over to the side, where the coach is collecting them. "Have your dad talk to my dad. Bring your shin guards and cleats on Wednesday and you can walk over to the field with us."

"We both live in Buckingham Heights," Xander says. "Right over there." He points. "Where are you?"

I don't want to say Deadly Gardens and I don't want to explain that I don't have cleats, so it's change-the-subject time. "Wait a minute, I have to do something." I start doing my victory dance. "I'm reliving that second-to-last goal we got. Wasn't that sweet?"

Langley laughs. "Musgrove gives me a perfect pass and I head it," he tells Xander, and he breaks into his victory dance, too.

Xander starts talking to Langley about how his dad is taking him to The Soccer Loft to get new cleats tonight and about how the cleats are designed with a combination of ultrathin kangaroo leather and microfiber. "The whole team should get them," Xander says. "We'd absolutely fry with those. Get your dad to bring you tonight just in case you make the team."

"Then we could talk our dads into stopping at Mama Bella's for chocolate gelato. My dad can't resist my poor boy face," Langley says to me, and makes this funny begging face.

I don't know what gelato is, but I say, "My dad can't resist mine, either," and I give him my funny begging face. "Me needo my gelato."

Langley laughs.

"Hey, maybe we'll see you tonight," Langley says. "I'll text you when we're going. What's your number?"

"My number? I lost my phone."

"Ouch. Get a new one, man."

I get the address of The Soccer Loft. It would be unbelievably cool to meet up with them later.

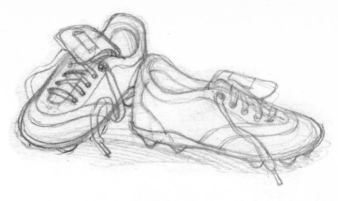

5.
DAD

You never really know what another person is thinking because most human beings are good actors. I'm an excellent actor. If somebody is talking about a dad, like "My dad is going to buy me some new cleats," I act like it's no big deal.

Sometimes I say my dad is away on a business trip. Sometimes I say my parents are divorced. The truth is I don't know what my dad looks like or where he is exactly. I know he's in jail somewhere in Delaware, but I stopped asking my mom about him because she just says, "He blew it big-time," and then she clamps her mouth shut.

Sometimes I try to send out good thoughts to him so that maybe he'll feel them and write me a letter or something. But sometimes I look out the window and feel bad thoughts streaming out of me like a virus on invisible lines. *I hate you. I hate you. I hate you. I hate you.*

Nothing more to say.

6.
CLEATS

"No!"

Her voice falls like an ax.

"Pretty please with whipped cream and three cherries . . ."

"No." My mom grabs her backpack. "Everybody needs to stop asking me for things." She throws Michael a look, which means they must have been fighting about something. When she turns her back, Michael sticks his tongue out at her.

I get down on my knees. "This is all I'm ever going to ask for. Ever."

"Trev, that lady who said she was gonna pay me

to take care of her kids? Now she's saying sorry, but she made other plans. I knocked on doors. I put up signs. Something'll come through, but we have to scrimp right now."

"I thought we moved 'cause this place was so cheap."

"It's cheaper than the old place, but it's still more than we'll be able to afford if I don't pull in more. I got us a couple of camping mattresses at Save the Children, but we need other stuff, too. I don't have enough to cover the cell phone bill this month. We can't even think about getting a regular phone."

Steam is practically coming out of Michael's ears he's so mad. "I need a new backpack." He lays each word down like a brick.

"Oh, that reminds me. I need a notebook for science." It's out of my mouth even though I know it's going to make her crazy.

"How come all my children were born without ears?" she screeches. "Michael, your backpack is fine. Trev, ask for a notebook at the office. They got supplies if you ask. And I'm sorry, but we can't get shin guards and cleats right now. Tish, be good. I'm going to the store to get some milk and put up some more signs. Stay in here." *Bam.* She's out the door and banging on it from the other side. "Lock this thing right now, Trev. And keep it locked."

Michael throws his shoe at the door. "Everybody says I'm garbage because I have a garbage backpack. Everybody has a superhero backpack but me."

Tish looks at me like she's going to cry, so I pick her up. Her diaper stinks.

"Okay, Little Man, keep your pants on. First of all, Mom is right. Your backpack is fine. How come I know? Because I've got the same one. It's not a Nike, but you don't see me complaining about that. It's better than fine. It's scorching red. Nice and plain. Tell those punks in kindergarten that's the best kind. What we need here is a strategy and some food. I'm so hungry I can't think."

Tish bounces in my arms. "Me wan food."

"No bounce bounce with that stinky diaper," I tell Tish. "Why can't you learn to use the potty?"

Michael grumbles, "I want a hot dog and root beer."

"*Me* woo bee!" Tish bounces again and whaps me on the head.

"Ow! No bang bang on people's heads, Little Cavewoman."

In the cupboard, there's one box of mac and cheese, one box of blue Jell-O, and one loaf of bread. All that's in the fridge is a bottle of chocolate syrup.

Without milk the mac and cheese won't taste right, so I make toast and drizzle chocolate syrup on it. To drink, I sprinkle blue Jell-O powder in sippy cups and add water. "Blue beer!" I hand it off. Michael actually grins and looks at me like I'm a high-class chef.

"Boo bee!" Tish says, and sucks her blue beer down.

"Booby! She said booby!" Michael's eyes get real big and we all crack up. As Tish drinks, her two little teeth turn blue, which makes me and Michael laugh even more.

"Okay, now we need a plan."

"For what?" Michael asks.

"To get on Mom's good side. She has a little extra money saved up. She calls it the 'emergency fund.' We need to talk her into borrowing some for shin guards and cleats."

I look around. I'd clean the place up, but Mom already scrubbed it—she even scrubbed the chalk drawing off the wall—and there's nothing to put away. We might as well be living inside a cardboard box.

"What about me getting a backpack?" Michael asks.

"If I get shin guards and cleats, I'll make this important team, and then I'll get spotted by a scout and become a famous soccer player, and I'll buy you whatever backpack you want."

"A superhero backpack?"

"Yep."

That gets him thinking. "We could make Momma a picture!" he says. "I made one but my teacher won't let me bring it home."

I don't know if a picture is really going to do the trick, but Michael is all excited now, and it's better than nothing. "Score one for Little Man!" I say. "Something to cover up that hole. It's a start anyway, right?"

All we got are a few pens and four colored pencils. What I really like best are markers. "Come on. Let's see if we can borrow some markers."

"Momma says stay here," Michael argues.

"She meant stay here most of the time. We're just gonna go quickly and come right back. It'll be a secret, so don't tell her."

I pick up Tish and we walk down the five flights. A couple of other kids are out, including Diamond. I'd ask her but she's sitting on the curb getting yelled at by some huge mean-looking man. She's definitely not singing now, if you know what I mean.

A big guy named Markus, who is in my Computer Applications class, is riding around and around the parking lot on a tiny bike, so I ask him if he's got any markers I could borrow because my little brother has this project he has to do.

Michael takes his thumb out of his mouth. "Trev, you're the one—"

"Don't worry, Michael, I'm gonna help you with it," I say real fast because I don't particularly want Markus knowing that we're planning to draw a pretty picture for our mommy.

"What do I get in return?" Markus asks.

"I could do your name on your shoe," I say. "Graffiti style."

I show him my name on my shoe.

"Nice." He nods. He takes us over to his building and up to the second floor, where he lives with his grandma. Never seen so much stuff jammed into one room.

"Man, you must be rich," I say.

"I get everything on discount," he says, and wiggles his fingers. "The five-finger discount."

I look at Michael to see if he knows that Markus is talking about stealing, but Michael just takes his thumb out of his mouth and whispers, "Smells good in here!"

"Grandma's spaghetti," Markus says. He pulls a drawer out of a desk and sets it on the dining table. It's like a whole dang store full of markers, some looking brand-new.

Mom would kill me if she knew I was borrowing markers from somebody who stole stuff, because that was one of my dad's problems. You can't take what you want, she says, you have to earn it.

Markus sets a pair of shoes on the table, even nicer than the ones he's got on. All white. "Show me first what it's gonna look like," he says.

He wants his first name so I design it on paper and make a deal that I can keep a handful of markers if I do one shoe.

He loves it.

"You got to do the other one now," Markus says.

"I'll do the other one for some paper. You got any bigger than this?"

"You don't even got paper? Man, where you come from? Shelter?"

That last comment ticks me off. At least I'm earning what I got, I want to say, but crossing the line with Markus would just get me in the kind of trouble I don't need.

I zip the lips and stay focused. Markus coughs up the paper, I do the other shoe, and we head back home.

Diamond is sitting on the curb, alone now, banging a plastic water bottle against the fence, saying over and over a word that Michael and Tish aren't supposed to even know exists.

Michael grabs my hand because he's scared, and you might think it's ridiculous to be scared of a skinny girl with a bad mouth, but you haven't seen Diamond. When she's messing around she's funny, but when she's mad her eyes look like they could cut you.

I try to help Michael laugh it off. "That bottle must've done something bad," I say, and Diamond looks up.

"It was a joke," I say.

"I know. I ain't stupid." She bangs it again.

"Who's she?" Michael whispers.

"She's a famous female recording artist from school," I say. "Her name is Diamond."

Diamond's hard face breaks into a smile. She holds the plastic bottle like a microphone and sings, *"Baby, baby, if you love me, set me free!"*

I guess she got her groove back. The truth is she's got a good voice, but I'm not about to tell her that because she'll think it's a marriage proposal or something.

"You trying out for the soccer team?" she asks.

"I'm trying out for a travel team. The Plague."

"With Xander and all them?" She practically spits. "The only reason they win is because their heads are five times bigger than everybody else's. Nobody can get around them."

Michael laughs at that one.

"Well," I say, "your head's so big when you go onstage the audience is going to have a heart attack."

"Oooh." She throws the bottle at me. "You better not come to the Stars Show because Celine and

I are trying out next week and I don't want your big huge head blocking the view for everybody else."

Michael laughs again.

"Hey, Little Man," I say. "Whose side are you on?"

"I'm in B23. What apartment you in?" Diamond asks.

"D513," Michael whispers before I can stop him. Great. Now Microphone Mouth knows exactly where I live.

Tish breaks away and heads for the Dumpster. The yellow tape is gone. I chase after her.

"Hey, Diamond," I call back. "You know if that baby is still alive?"

"Ain't you got no TV?" she asks.

"The 103-inch plasma screen I ordered hasn't come yet."

"Ha. Ha. He's in that intensive care place over at Saint Francis."

"Charlie?" Michael whispers.

"Yeah."

"We got his name in our window," Michael tells her.

Michael finally gets brave enough to talk and he decides to tell her about writing Charlie's name in our windowsill.

She wants to know what he means. I just say nothing and tell Michael we have to go home.

"Me up," Tish says.

"Okay, Little Cavewoman." I pick up Tish and start heading home.

Diamond calls after us. "You know why I'm gonna fail math? Because I sit behind your big head and I can't see the teacher!"

As soon as we get home, Michael makes me rewrite Charlie's name in blue chalk because it's fading, and then he and Tish want to draw a picture, so we do one together.

I love how when I draw, I'm not thinking about anything else. I'm just focusing all my good feelings into the juice of the pen and it's flowing out onto the paper. There's something real peaceful about it.

"Momma's gonna like this," Michael says. "It makes us look imported."

"Important."

"Put Charlie in it," Michael says. "In a real soft blanket."

Mom's going to wonder who the heck Charlie is, but that's okay.

I want to hang the picture over the hole in the wall, but Michael says it has to go on the outside of the door so it's the first thing Mom sees.

7.
PIECES

Tish and Michael are sleeping by the time I hear the key in the lock.

Mom's got two bags of groceries and a look on her face like she's been chewing dirt. She's trying to close the door with her foot.

"Wait!" I grab the door. "What happened to the picture?"

"What picture?"

"We made a picture for you and put it on the door."

Taped to the door is a little corner of the paper, but the rest of it is gone.

"Take this, Trev! My arm's about to fall off."

There's something balled up by the stairwell. I run down and pick it up. It's our picture. I uncrumple it, and pieces of it come apart in my hands. Somebody tore our picture off our door. Why would anybody do that?

"Trev . . ."

What's the point? Why destroy something of somebody else's just for the sake of destroying it?

"Trev . . . what are you doing?"

"We made a picture to get you in a good mood."

She sighs and hands me a bag. "That was nice. Did you give Michael and Tish some dinner?"

"Yeah. Mom, I was thinking we could borrow just a little out of the emergency fund for those cleats and then I'd pay—"

"Honey, you're not listening. We cannot afford anything right now."

I wish I had my own room with a door so I could slam it.

8.
SHOE BUSINESS

Morning slaps me across the face.

Wake up, Musgrove. Get moving.

Michael is throwing a fit because last night's plan didn't produce a new backpack for him. He thought he was going to wake up and find one under his pillow and is mad at me because it didn't happen. What am I . . . the Backpack Fairy?

I got problems of my own. At the bus stop, I ask everybody if they have cleats or shin guards I can borrow.

"You should go to Save the Children," Juan suggests. "Secondhand. I got mine there."

"Oooh, yeah," Diamond says. "Everything is like a dollar. I could show you where it is."

"Secondhand?" Markus says. "More like third-hand or fourth-hand. My grandpa won't even wear clothes from there and he's dead."

Diamond hits him.

An eighth grader walks up. "Hey, Markus. Where'd you get the shoes, man?"

Markus is wearing the shoes with my creations on them.

"I did those!" I say.

"No way." He's checking them out.

"Do yours for a dollar . . ."

The guy nods. "Definitely. If I had a dollar on me."

He was like free advertising. "You hear that?" I ask around. "Now, come on! Which of you here is going to be the next one to get a graffiti-style deluxe one-of-a-kind shoe design?"

"Do me," Diamond says, and holds out her flip-flop.

"Watch out, man," Markus says. "I think she's in love with you."

Diamond hits Markus again, and her friend Celine says, "Ooooh, it's true."

"Can you do me the Nike logo?" Juan asks. "Right here." He points.

Markus snorts. "You want your knockoffs to look like the real deal."

I cut in fast before Juan can change his mind. "Hey, I can make 'em look like they're made out of diamonds if you got a dollar."

"Diamonds!" Microphone Mouth screams. "Make me a logo with diamonds that says Diamond!"

Juan digs around in his backpack and puts together one dollar in change just as the bus pulls up.

It takes the whole bus ride for me to complete the job because I can only draw whenever the bus is at a stop sign. I add tight little lines around the edges of the design so it looks like it was stitched on with thread.

Juan goes crazy when I'm done. "Man, they look just like I bought 'em that way."

Diamond is hanging over the seat, watching. "Come on. Do my logo," she begs. "I'll get you a dollar later."

"Your girlfriend wants you to do her," Markus laughs.

"Shut up, Mark*ass*!" Diamond gets up and hits him again, and the bus driver yells at her to sit down.

She sticks her bruised-up arm in my face. "Do it on my arm like a tattoo."

"A diamond tattoo is the only kind of diamond you're ever gonna get," Markus says.

"*Stolen* diamond is the only kind you're ever gonna get," Diamond snaps back.

"Diamond got suspended last year," Markus tells me. "Twice."

"Well, he got arrested," she says.

Juan is the first off the bus, strutting his new shoes. "Come on, Trevor, it's Tuesday. Cinnamon rolls." Everybody from the bus is heading to the cafeteria for free breakfast.

"Nah," I say. "I don't like cinnamon rolls."

"Don't like cinnamon rolls?" Markus exclaims. "Get yours and give it to me."

"For a dollar," I say.

"Aw, man, you're hurting me." Markus laughs, and I keep walking. "I'm a growing boy!" Markus calls after me. "I need my cinnamon rolls!"

Everybody laughs because Markus is already the size of an eighteen-wheeler.

I climb the stairs, turn the corner, and see Xander at his locker.

"Hey, did you get your kangaroo cleats?" I ask.

He nods and smiles. "You wouldn't believe how sweet they are. Hey, Stephanie!" From the bottom of his locker he pulls out a Eurogear catalog and holds it up so she can see. Xander's on the cover, standing in a field, looking all fierce, with one foot on a soccer ball. "I told you I had one for you!"

Stephanie comes over, and Xander autographs it for her. She goes crazy.

I can't believe I know somebody who is on the cover of a catalog. Maybe if I make the team, he'll tell me how he did it.

"Hey, Ben!" he calls out to somebody. "Later, Musgrove."

At lunchtime, Markus sees me first and waves me over to the Deadly Gardens table, but I make sure to be looking all casually the other way—I'll have to tell him later that I didn't see him. I saunter toward the Summit table. Langley is saying something and everybody is laughing. I catch his eye.

"Hey, Musgrove!" Langley calls me over.

That's all you need—just a little invitation to get things going. I set my tray down at the table, and Xander says, "How can you eat that garbage?"

Nobody at this table has a school lunch, which makes me look like a fool. But that's okay because I know what to do in a situation like this. As my mom says, people may try to make you look like a fool, but that doesn't mean you have to feel like one. "Yum," I say, and take a big sniff of my free lunch. "Tray-o-McTrash."

Langley laughs.

"He's dissing your name, McCloud," one of the guys says.

I forgot about Langley's last name.

"No way," Langley says. "McSpeak is a sign of respect, right?" He grabs one of my French fries. Langley is my favorite kind of guy—a guy who can take a joke.

Xander starts back up with a conversation

they must have been having about voice-mail messages. "Anyway, mine says, 'I'm not really here, so don't really leave a message.'"

Langley laughs. "Ben's message is hilarious. It sounds like either he just woke up or he's drunk." He does an impression, and Ben, this guy at the end of the table, laughs his head off.

I take a chance. "Mine says, 'Please leave a message after the tone.' And then I do the sound of a really long fart."

Everybody laughs.

"I thought you lost your phone," Xander says.

"Yeah, it *was* my message before I lost it."

Xander asks what brand it was.

"Hey, speaking of phones." I finesse the subject in a new direction. "What was that you were playing for everybody on your phone yesterday?"

The whole table starts laughing again. "The funniest goal," Xander says. "I was at the MCS Elite camp in England . . ."

"And he shot this goal and it hit the goalie right in the face." Langley stands up and goes into the slo-mo routine that he was doing when I first saw him. It's like he's the goalie, and the ball is coming at him and he gets hit in the face and his whole head wobbles like it's going to fly off. It's so funny I almost spurt my milk right out of my nose.

Ben tells a story about a funny goal that a guy made at the University of Maryland camp he went to.

"What camps did you do this summer?" Xander asks me.

I'm not sure how to finesse myself out of this one. Michael and Tish and I camped out in McDonald's Playland one afternoon and threw plastic balls at each other and that was about as fun as it got. "This summer?" Just when I'm trying to think up what to say, the wind blows a little luck my way. Actually, it's big luck. The tallest kid in the school, the guy who was the scoring champ for last year's basketball team, according to Langley, walks over and asks me if I'm the "graffiti guy" because he wants to buy a design. *Swish!* Just like that I go from being a nobody to being Graffiti Guy. Fill up the limo, baby, here I come.

Of course, I play it very casually. "Sure I can do

that," I say, and then I casually raise my price.

He gets out his wallet and puts his foot up saying, "Man, trust me. You don't want me to take these puppies off."

"Yeah. I can smell 'em from here." I joke like it's a drag, but I'm excited. As I draw, Langley comes around so he can watch.

Xander isn't impressed, though. He keeps talking about how much his new cleats cost—and the shoes he's wearing—and how he wouldn't mess them up by drawing on them. When I'm done, everybody else goes crazy over my design, and Langley asks me to do his name. I do it and it looks totally high quality, if I do say so myself. I have as much business as I can handle during the next fifteen minutes, and then the bell rings.

Nothing like the feeling of new bills in your pocket. If everything's a dollar, I got enough for shin guards, cleats, and maybe even a jersey at Save the Children.

"You know where to find me," I tell the ones who are still waiting.

9.
UNDERGROUND INTELLIGENCE

Mr. Ferguson calls me up to his desk before class starts.

Now he's going to tell me I'm in the wrong class.

He pulls a piece of crumpled paper out of his grade book. It's the entry I did yesterday of the meadow mushroom. "I found this on the floor, Mr. Musgrove. On the floor. One of the purposes of a notebook is to keep your notes together. This is the most important project of the entire semester. Do you understand?"

I nod.

He hands me a second sheet. It's the drawing I did of him labeled as a fungi. "I believe this is yours, too."

Now I'm ready to crawl under a rock.

"You have your notebook?"

"My mom is taking me to get one tonight," I say quickly.

"Mr. Musgrove . . ." He leans toward me and pulls his glasses down. "I want to believe you." He stares like he's able to see through my lie all the way down to my roots. Some teachers are waiting for you to mess up, but Mr. Ferguson seems like he wants to believe me, which makes me feel even worse.

"I'll have the notebook tomorrow." I fold up the Mr. Fungus picture. "And I'm sorry about this one."

He leans back and pushes his glasses up. "I could take it as a compliment." He smiles and his freckles dance. "It all depends on how you meant it."

"Total compliment," I say. "I never met a fungus I didn't like."

Mr. Ferguson laughs.

Trevor Finesse Musgrove gets the goal.

The rest of the class is in by now, so Mr. Ferguson grabs his cap and walking stick and says, "Don't bother sitting down, Mr. Musgrove. Let us perambulate to the egress!"

Everybody looks confused.

"*Walk* to the *exit*," he says.

"Are we perambulating to the egress for a foray with our utensils?" Langley asks.

"Excellent supposition, Mr. McCloud."

Langley and I both do funny walks toward the egress at the same time, which cracks everybody up and proves how much we think alike. Ferguson is way ahead, so we keep the funny perambulations going out the door and over to the side of the school, where there is a small greenhouse. In front of the greenhouse, there are two little trees in big pots. One tree is twice the size of the other.

"I think it's time to cease our perambulating and ponder over the botanical uprisings in these clay vessels!" Langley whispers.

Stephanie hears it and hits him. "Stop making fun!" But she's laughing, and Langley isn't being mean. You can only make fun of people you don't like, and how could you not like a fungus-loving, vocabularically dazzling leprechaun?

Mr. Ferguson taps his walking stick against each pot. "I planted these saplings six weeks ago when they were both exactly the same height. They are both saplings from the same kind of tree—a maple. I have given them the same amount of sunlight, the same amount of water. Who can guess why one is taller and healthier than the other?"

Hands go up.

Mr. Ferguson calls on Xander, who guesses that it has something to do with something called mycelium.

The teacher's eyes light up. He's like a kindergartner who is all excited about a new toy and wants everybody in the whole world to be excited, too. "Smart thinking, Mr. Pierce. You obviously did the reading. Mycelium, singular. Mycelia, plural. Who can explain what a mycelium is?"

"It's an organism," Langley says. "A fungus. It lives in the ground or inside dead wood."

"Bingo! Give that man one hundred thousand dollars!"

Langley holds out his hand, and Mr. Ferguson pulls a dried mushroom out of his pocket and gives it to him.

Langley looks at it and says, "Thank you very mush."

Everybody laughs.

"Mr. Musgrove, can you dig up an entire mycelium and show it to me?" Mr. Ferguson asks.

Is he asking me to do it or asking me *if* I can do it? I don't know what a mycelium is. Dang. Think quick. I smile and hold out my hand. "Give me a hundred thousand dollars and I can dig up *mycel*anything."

Score! Everybody's laughing.

"Um, not really!" Mosquito Boy jumps in, obviously lacking the humor gene. "It's like a web, a massive bunch of really thin rootlike things all tangled up and connected to whatever it's growing in, like dirt. Mushrooms are just a tiny part of the mycelium that pops out. There was that picture in the book of somebody pulling a mushroom carefully out of the ground, and you can see the little white threads hanging off the bottom."

Looks like everybody did the homework but me.

Mr. Ferguson nods. "Interesting way to describe it! Yes, there is mycelium in this dirt." He points to the bigger sapling. "Because I introduced it to this soil." He points to the smaller sapling. "This is the same potting soil without mycelium. Remember that when I started, both trees were the same size. So what can you hypothesize, Mr. Musgrove?"

"The mycelium helps plants grow," I guess.

"Yes. Certain fungi help plants grow. How?"

"By being nice?"

Everybody laughs.

Mr. Ferguson smiles and looks at me and Langley. "The jokes just pop out of you two, don't they?"

"Like mushrooms popping out of dirt," I say.

He laughs. "Well, let's do a little demonstration. Imagine Ms. Taylor here is a little tree in a big forest." He motions for Stephanie Taylor to come up to the front, which she is loving. She's the kind of girl who looks like she was born to be in the spotlight. Perfect hair. Perfect smile. Perfect everything. "Be a tree," Mr. Ferguson says.

She raises her arms and smiles.

Some people clap and Xander and Langley whistle.

"Almost. You're a sad little thirsty tree," Mr. Ferguson says, bringing her arms down so that she droops. "Better! Now imagine over here is a river and near the river are big healthy trees." He positions Langley, Xander, and Sam. Langley stomps into place and starts flexing his biceps like he's in a bodybuilding competition. Mr. Ferguson rolls his eyes. "I have a class full of hams!" he says, but he's getting a kick out of it. "All right. There is a drought in the region. These trees are close enough to the river to get water and nutrients through their root systems. How does poor Ms. Taylor get what she needs?"

"The mycelium?" Mosquito Boy calls out.

"Right." Mr. Ferguson tells the rest of us—the ones who aren't trees—to lie down and connect with fingers or feet to another person. "Don't be shy! Put your hand on somebody's shoulder and your foot touching somebody else. Everybody has to connect somehow. A mycelium is like a network of microscopic threads."

I'm right in the middle so I've got a girl on one side and a boy on the other. No way we're holding hands or anything, so I bend my arms and touch my elbows against their arms. Then I reach down and touch my foot to a girl's shoulder. At the same time the guy who is lying down above my head touches me with his shoe.

"This class should come with extra shampoo," I say.

Mr. Ferguson laughs. "Okay. You are just a small part of the massive mycelium that is running under the soil of this great forest. And when I say massive, here's what I mean . . . in one cubic inch of soil, there's eight miles' worth of you all tangled together. Try to imagine that. You grow quickly and you spread throughout the soil, joining strand to strand, making the soil nice and spongy so that it holds water and nutrients better and creates conditions that are perfect for growing trees and food."

"Thank you, fungus," Langley says.

Mr. Ferguson laughs.

I love this class. I'd love school if every class came outside and pretended to be a fungus. Smells so good out here. Feels good, too. Just lying down in the grass. Above me the sky is like a canvas that has been painted the most perfect shade of blue, and I want to reach up and write my name in the sky. *Trevor Musgrove.* I'd like to have a skywriting business and write people's names in the sky. When the wind blows, each letter will billow and stretch, like the name is alive.

Mr. Ferguson continues and his voice takes on this low, calm tone, like he's hypnotizing us. "You are the fungus. Now the remarkable thing is that you are not just connected to one another, you happen to be a mycorrhizal fungus, a fungus that has a beneficial relationship with a plant, so you are also connected to the roots of these trees. Go ahead, the people closest to the trees, connect to them."

The girls near the boys are giggling because they have to touch one another. It's like we've all made this invisible agreement to act like little kids again, in a fun way, because it just feels so good to be out of jail.

As soon as everybody is in place, Mr. Ferguson goes on. "You have a certain kind of intelligence."

"Because we're in the Summit program!" Langley says, and everybody laughs again.

"No. Because you're a mycorrhizal fungus. You are listening for and reacting to signals from your partners, the trees. The parts of you closest to Ms. Taylor pick up her distress signal. Ms. Taylor, give them a distress signal."

Like a maiden in distress, Stephanie says, "Help! I need water!"

The class laughs.

"Go ahead and pass the message on."

The students closest to Stephanie pass the message from one to the other. "She needs water." We're like a maze, so the message spreads out quickly. "She needs water. She needs water." It becomes a hum that travels to me and then I get to pass it on. "She needs water." Finally it travels all the way to the big trees.

"I got water, right?" Langley says.

"Yes. Because you're closer to the river. So what are you going to do?" Mr. Ferguson says.

"Pass some back to her." Langley starts to make like he's going to spit and Stephanie mock-screams and covers her hair.

"Think of another way, please," Mr. Ferguson says.

"Okay," Langley says. "Here's some water," he taps the girl who is connected to him who taps the student who is connected to her and says, "Here's some water." The imaginary water travels back through the class, slower because it's being tapped now from person to person, one at a time. "Here's some water. Here's some water."

On my back in the soft grass, I wait to see if the message will come to me. I hope it does because I want to pass it on. I know everybody's feeling the same way. We're all totally into it. Maybe it's because we're all connected, but it's like I can feel how thirsty Stephanie is, like it's life or death even though we are all playing a game.

The message gets closer, and then the girl next to me gets it and giggles. "Here's some water," she says to me, and my arm gets ready because it's our elbows touching, and I'm racking my brain for a good joke to make. Then, for some reason, she reaches over and taps the back of my hand with her fingertips. *Tap.* I can almost feel droplets of water there.

The straightest path to Stephanie goes through my feet, so I close my eyes and imagine sending the water from my hand, through my body, to my foot. As lightly as I can I tap the other girl's shoulder with my foot. "Here's some water."

I keep my eyes closed, but I can hear the water being passed from person to person. There's a hush when the water arrives to Stephanie. I imagine her like a tree, drinking in the water through her roots. I imagine how good it must feel to drink the water after being so thirsty. I imagine the water rising up in her and seeping into her leaves.

"Thanks, everybody," she says, and some people laugh, but my throat closes up because I think about Charlie.

How come there can be a mycelium in the ground that will bring water to the roots of a thirsty tree, and there can be nothing under a baby but a bed of garbage? He must have been thirsty. He must have been waiting for someone to come, even if he couldn't put it into words.

I open my eyes, and the sky above me is so blue it hurts.

"Mr. Musgrove?"

Everybody is looking at me.

I sit up.

"Diana was asking if a mycorrhizal fungus could be considered 'good.' Are there good fungi and bad fungi? Should we talk about fungi in moral terms?"

Mosquito Boy comes to my rescue. "I think the mycorrhizal fungus isn't doing this because it feels sorry for the tree or feels obligated to help the tree, but it passes on the water kind of automatically? Because it's all part of the biological design? The fungus gets something and gives something."

"Well said. Of course the fungus and the tree aren't actually talking to each other with words the way we did. But you can think of this fungus like a mother, trying to nurture her offspring and the food chain that provides nutrition for her children."

"Are you calling my mom a fungus?" Langley asks.

Mr. Ferguson laughs.

"So there is a mycelium under us right here?" Lydia asks.

Mr. Ferguson nods.

"How do you know for sure?" I ask.

He smiles and points to the grass behind Sam with his walking stick. "What do you see?"

Sam gets out of the way. There's a mushroom.

"Proof!" Mr. Ferguson says. "Now I want you to sit down where you are and try to draw a depiction of what we just acted out. Then write down your comments and add more from the book. Remember: I want to read your thoughts, not just the facts."

As we're working, Ferguson strolls around. "Now you can all put down on your work résumés that you have worked as fungi!"

Somebody asks how he knows so much about mushrooms.

"I'm a mycologist," he explains. "I got my degree in the study of mushrooms."

I ask how he became interested in mushrooms in the first place.

"I grew up in a very poor part of West Virginia," he says. "Believe it or not we picked mushrooms for dinner. I became interested in identifying them because once I brought home the wrong kind and my whole family died."

All the pencils stop moving.

He laughs. "Just kidding about the dying part. Nobody died, but once I did pick a bad one, and we all had diarrhea for days. It's not always easy to identify which mushrooms are good for you and which are bad for you. And I have heard about fatal mushroom poisoning, which is why you all should never eat anything you pick."

"Do you eat what you pick?"

"Yes, but I've been studying mushrooms for decades."

He strolls on, swinging his stick.

West Virginia? I didn't know there were mushroom-eating, hypnotizing, freckle-faced, leprechauns with little white Afros perambulating around in West Virginia.

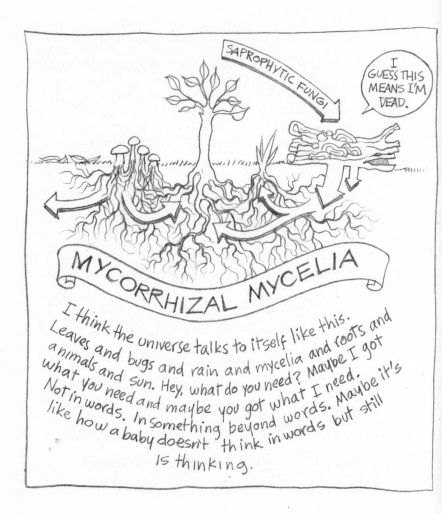

10.
JUGGLING

In P.E., Xander and I get on the same team. We're supposed to be warming up on our own while Stevins works with teams at the other end of the field. Javier—another good player who is built like a bulldog—is juggling. Solid skills, especially for somebody who likes to play keeper. No problem getting to forty, but he loses it before fifty. He tries again.

Xander watches him and then says to me that he can juggle to one hundred, no problem.

Javier loses his rhythm. "Is that a challenge?" He throws Xander the ball.

Bam. Xander pops it off his chest and catches it

with the top of his foot. *Bam. Bam.* Juggles from foot to thigh to foot—

"Dang, I can do that," Markus shouts. Everybody laughs because they all know he can't.

Xander keeps going. Spotlight on him. Shoes gleaming. Everybody starts chanting out the count: thirty-nine, forty. . . .

He loses the ball at sixty-two, and his face turns bright red. He picks it up and tries to start again.

"No way," Javier says. "You didn't say you'd get to one hundred eventually. You said get to one hundred, period. And I guess you didn't."

"Still, I fried you," Xander says.

Diamond grabs the ball and throws it to me. "You do it."

A couple of other guys egg me on, too.

"Go ahead, Musgrove," Xander says.

The ball feels good. Just the right amount of air. *Bam. Bam.* Juggling is something I am really good at because you don't need a field to juggle, or even a team. You can juggle anywhere, even a parking lot with broken glass in it.

I hit twenty, and Diamond starts in with this

song, *"You got it, oh baby, yeah you got it,"* to the same rhythm I'm making and people start counting to the beat. . . . I feel my face getting hot. . . . I am in this sweet zone, just me and the ball. . . . Sixty, sixty-one, sixty-two . . . It's like the ball is connected to me, like it wants to keep coming back. . . . Seventy, seventy-one, seventy-two . . . eighty!

Coach Stevins's whistle blows, and the ball hits the side of my foot and bounces away. The girls are cheering and people are clapping.

"Man, you could've kept going," Javier says.

Feels so good! I'm about to break into my victory dance when I look up and realize I crossed Xander's invisible line. His eyes are burning. He hates me for beating him. I should have come close, but not shown him up. I have to save the day quickly with one of my jokes, but Diamond's laugh flies through the air like a knife. She says, "Trev beat you and he looked like he wasn't even trying." She gets in one more before I can even blink. "I guess if you got talent you don't need fancy shoes."

"Okay, people, let's get going!" Coach Stevins blows his whistle again.

"I got lucky," I try to say, but Xander won't look at me.

During the game, I make sure to pass every ball I get to Xander. Quality passes. Xander scores five goals. I don't take a single shot, just keep feeding them to him.

Javier, who's our goalie, notices. "Nice assists," he says to me when I'm nearby.

Twice Coach Stevins yells from the sidelines, "Play as a team, people!" In this case, *people* has to mean *Xander*.

"Great game," I say to Xander when the whistle blows.

Xander doesn't say a word.

Langley catches up with us when we're walking in. "Did you guys win?"

"Yeah, but I could have used you," Xander says. "It was like I was alone out there."

I can't believe what I'm hearing.

"My team fried, too," Langley says. "That little Juan guy has got the moves. Hey, see you tomorrow, Musgrove. Remember, tryouts after school."

Xander says, "Yeah. See you tomorrow, Mushroom."

I could say something. I could say a whole lot of something, but I don't. My mom says when people put you down, rise above it.

11.
SAVE THE CHILDREN

On the bus ride home, Diamond sits behind me and puts her arm over the seat between me and Juan. She jiggles the four quarters she has in her hand and begs for me to logo up her name. "Right here." She turns her forearm.

I don't answer.

She keeps bugging me until Juan says, "Man, just do it so she shuts up."

"No."

"I'll show you where Save the Children is," she says even though she already told me how to get there.

Markus grins. "The lovebirds are going shopping together."

I've had it. "Keep your mouth shut—"

"What are you gonna do?" Markus stands up.

"Sit down right now," the bus driver yells.

"Chill, man," Juan whispers. "It ain't worth it."

Rise above it. I close my eyes.

"I was just doing a favor," Diamond grumbles.

As soon as the bus arrives at Deadly Gardens, I take off running. Diamond says it's a five-minute walk to Save the Children; it's more like a fifteen-minute run. I'm going to get some cleats and shin guards and I'm going to get on The Plague and prove to Xander that I'm the kind of guy he wants on his team and everything is going to get back on track.

The place is crowded with merchandise, but they have only five pairs of cleats, three of which are Michael's size, and none of which required the killing of a kangaroo. Quickly I try on the only two that are anywhere near close to my size. One is too big and the other is a little too small. The small ones pinch my feet, but even with two pairs of socks I am afraid the big ones will fly off. I take the smaller cleats, find the only pair of shin guards in the place, and run up to the counter, where an Indian girl with a long black ponytail is working. She has on blue gloves and is sorting men's underwear from a large garbage bag into bins labeled small, medium, large, and extra large.

Everything is *not* a dollar, as Diamond said, and I'm two dollars short. I put on my best smile and pull out my money. "If you give me a discount, I'll give you a valuable prize."

She adjusts her scarf and narrows her eyes. "What is the prize?"

"My respect and your own satisfaction in helping out a rising soccer star. A valuable prize, indeed."

She points to a poster board with words scribbled on it. NO BARGAINING. ALL SALES FINAL. NO RETURNS.

"But this is Save the Children." I smile. "You're supposed to save me."

She doesn't look up, doesn't even crack a smile.

"Please don't make me perambulate to the egress empty-handed!"

She gives me a look, like I'm an alien who just walked in from outer space.

Clearly my vocabularic genius isn't doing it. I have to try another tactic. "I could work for it. I could do that." I point to the big bag of not-so-whitey tighties.

Bingo. She leans forward. "Let me see those."

I hand her the cleats and shin guards and she takes her time, looking at them as if they hold the answer.

Hurry.

"You're only two dollars off?" she asks.

"Yep."

"You'd do this whole bag?"

"Yes, I would."

"The manager won't like it. . . . He's coming back in fifteen minutes."

"I can do it in ten."

She smiles and picks up her soda. "Deal."

I take over her job, wishing I had gloves, while she sits back and sips her soda and talks on her cell phone. I work as quickly as I can, glancing at the clock. Nine minutes pass and I still have more to go. I work faster. Three minutes later, I toss the last one in the large bin. She hands me the shin guards and the cleats.

I stuff the shin guards in my backpack and swing the cleats around, singing, *"I got it. I got it. Oh, yeah. Oh, yeah. I got it."*

I sound like Diamond. Oh, well, I can't help it.

The clerk laughs.

"I'm going to try out for a soccer team and be MVP and get my picture on the cover of a magazine," I call back to her in one breath as I hustle to the egress.

"See you, famous boy," she says.

"Hey! I need a notebook with no lines. Got any?"

"Try Rite Aid."

It's 5:20. I take off running. My mom is probably having a heart attack, but she'll be proud of me as soon as I tell her what I did. She can't say no to the team now. What's there to say no to? I sing as I jog, *"I got it. I got it. Oh, yeah. Oh, yeah. I got it."*

A man waiting for the bus gives me a funny look as I pass by, but I keep singing and swinging my cleats. *"I got it. I got it. Oh, yeah. Oh, yeah. I got it."*

I pass by a print shop just as a guy is bringing out a box of paper to the recycling bin on the street.

"You recycling that?" I ask.

He nods. "Typo."

Quality paper—creamy and thick—with a business name and address on the top and the rest blank.

"Can I have it?"

The guy shrugs. "Sure."

I take the box and keep running. *"I got it. I got it. Oh, yeah. Oh, yeah. I got it."*

An African woman with a bright green head scarf smiles broadly and calls out, "Boy, whatever you got, I want!"

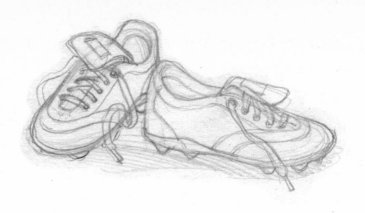

12.
WAYNE

I run up the stairwell, but on the fourth floor I stop. The air smells worse than usual, like somebody peed, and something just doesn't feel right. When I make the turn to go up to the fifth floor, I see a man sitting in the doorway that leads to the fifth floor hallway.

He's the big man who was yelling at Diamond—I think it's Derrick, her stepdad or her mom's boyfriend—sleeping, propped up against the door frame. She said she doesn't like going home if he's there. I can see why. He has an empty bottle in one hand, and the concrete around him is wet. His face is heavy and sweaty and looks like it was made out of mud and he has on the biggest, muddiest boots I've ever seen.

I have no idea why he's in my building. All I want to do is get home, but in order to do that I have to step over him. What if he's not really asleep? What if he's pretending and just when I get near him, he opens his eyelids and reaches out and grabs me? I stand for a few seconds, hearing music coming from somebody's place on the floor above me. The man's face is so still, he doesn't look like he's breathing. Maybe he's dead?

The stink is evil. I tiptoe closer, holding my breath.

Stay asleep, Mudman.

I step over the man's hand, the one holding the empty bottle. I have two more steps to go and then I'll be clear. A door slams down the hall. The man's arm jumps. The bottle crashes. I run.

Our door is locked. I bang on it and try to get my key out of my backpack at the same time. Behind, I can hear Mudman cursing.

My mom lets me in—Tish balanced on one

hip—and I quickly close and lock the door. I made it.

"Where have you been? What's going on? Why are you out of breath?" She sees the cleats. "Where did you get those?"

Sometimes my mom is as fast with her mouth as I am with my feet. I try to explain everything and catch my breath at the same time and when I describe The Plague, she sets Tish down. "You can't go out for that kind of team, Trev."

"Why not? All I needed was these and I got them. The tryouts are tomorrow and—"

"Trev, those teams cost money. There's fees and stuff. What about the school team?"

"I can earn my own money."

"Not that kind of money. Tish, let go of my leg."

"How do you know?"

"Listen to me, how are you getting to the practices and the games?"

"I'll take the bus. The Ride-On lets you ride free with a school ID."

"What if the games are far away? The bus doesn't just go anywhere you want to go."

Her voice is aimed at me and just keeps hitting like a punch. I don't want to listen. I am going to try out for the team tomorrow; I don't care what she says.

"Get back here. Where are you going?"

Maybe Juan has a ball and we can shoot on each other.

"Trev." She stops me. "Tish, go play with Michael." She pulls me into the bedroom and whispers, "Listen. I tracked Wayne down."

Wayne is Michael and Tish's dad. He moved in when Michael was born, and I liked him all right. Sometimes I would even pretend he was my dad. I never told anybody that. I'd just think it to myself. But after Tish was born, he was always getting headaches and one day he was gone.

"Is he coming back?" I ask.

"No," she says quickly. "I called him for child support. This time he actually says he has it and he'll come by. I think Social Services is on his back. I was hoping he'd come already, but he hasn't."

"What's that got to do with me?"

"I'm going to the Fry Factory about a job because

they said that's when the manager would be there. I don't want this to fall in your lap, but he might come when I'm gone so I wanted you to know." She tugs a rubber band off her wrist and pulls her hair back into a ponytail so tight it stretches the skin by her eyes. "I'm not telling Michael and Tish anything. Tish is too little anyway, and I don't want to get Michael's hopes up thinking he's got some daddy coming to rescue him. So if Wayne comes, don't answer or anything. I told him to just slip the money under the door. If you see it, grab it so Tish doesn't flush it down the potty or anything."

She asks about homework, and I snap and ask her how to do my Computer Applications homework without a computer.

She just gets mad at the teacher for assuming that everybody's got one, which does me no good. She shows me what we should eat for dinner if she's late and says to make sure to give Tish and Michael baths and then she is out the door.

Michael takes his thumb out of his mouth and says, "Trev, you can't make me take a bath."

"Stop being a baby," I snap. "You're just afraid you'll go down the drain."

Michael glares at me. "I hate you."

"Well, you stink," I say. "This whole place stinks."

Tish waddles over and tugs on my shorts and says, "Bubbie!" which is her word for bubbles, which means that she wants to take a bath. Tish is like a mermaid. She loves the water.

"Leave me alone," I say. "I'm in a bad mood." I go into the bedroom, push a load of dirty clothes off the mattress, and sit down. "How come we don't have any clean clothes?" I say to myself, but Michael answers.

"She said them washing machines down there are busted. We got to go to a laundry place."

Tish waddles in with her big diaper, puts her face close to mine, and looks at me fiercely. "Me bubbie now!"

In spite of how mad I am and how sorry for myself I feel, I have to laugh. "You think you're tough, huh, Little Cavewoman?" I ask.

She nods, all seriousness, and I laugh again and tickle her. She's so little and cute. I don't understand how anybody could give her up.

If Wayne comes, I'll tell him that Tish has

outgrown her crybaby stage and that Michael doesn't wet himself every night the way he used to. Wayne will see how cute they are and decide to stay. He'll bring money so Mom won't have to worry and then I can be on the team. "Let's order pizza," Wayne will say, and Mom will come home and see everybody sitting around the table eating and laughing and she'll be happy.

"Bath time," I say. "We have to get ready."

"No," Michael says.

"Little guys who stink never ever get new backpacks. If you get clean something good might happen."

I run water in the tub and peel off Tish's diaper. "You stink worse than Michael!" I say, picking her up.

"Me stinkie!" She laughs and kicks her little legs in the air, and then I slip her into the water and she sits, happy as a duck. I squeeze some dish soap into the tub and turn on some more water until it bubbles and foams.

"Bubbies!" she says, and splashes the water.

Michael comes in and stands there, looking at

the water, sucking his thumb, wanting to go in but scared.

"It's okay, Little Man. Nothing's going to happen." I scoop up a handful of bubbles and lay them on his arm. "See. Feels good."

Michael climbs in carefully, like if he steps in the wrong spot, a trapdoor will open and he'll get sucked in.

"Here's a boat." I set a toothpaste box on the surface of the water in front of Michael. They watch it float. I would like to be a little kid again. Little kids don't have very big problems.

"Me wan boat," Tish says, and slaps the water.

"Okay," I say. "I'll be back in one second. No messing around. Okay?"

I go into the kitchen and get an empty Jell-O box out of the trash. My mom's orange shoe box is on top of the refrigerator, which makes me think about Charlie. I wonder who found him and how that person felt. I imagine that I'm the one walking past the Dumpster and hearing a sound. I imagine lifting the box out, feeling the weight of something living in my hands. I imagine opening it and seeing a perfect little baby inside crying. *It's okay, Charlie. You're safe now.*

I notice silence. There's no sound coming from the bathroom, no splashing or talking or giggling or arguing or screaming. My blood goes cold. My heart starts pounding. Then Michael screams.

I run into the bathroom, expecting—I don't even want to say what I'm expecting—but Michael is holding up the soggy pieces of the toothpaste-box boat.

"It sunk!" Michael says.

Relief washes over me like a huge wave.

"It's okay." I take the wet box and throw it in the trash. My heart is still pounding.

"Me wan boat," Tish says.

I set the Jell-O box on a cloud of suds and blow gently. The little box boat drifts toward Tish, and she looks at me as if I'm a hero. "It's not going to last, okay, Tish? It's going to get wet and sink. Don't go crying when that happens."

"What's on your hand?" Michael points to the *H* that I wrote on my hand.

"Oh! *H* stands for science homework," I say. My reminder. "Thanks, Little Man." I bring in the box of paper I picked up from the print shop and my science book so I can do my homework and keep an eye on them at the same time.

"I got homework, too," Michael says, even though it isn't true.

"Me wan home ork," Tish says.

I laugh. "Trust me. You don't want home ork."

In between two pieces of stiff cardboard, I put a stack of the paper with the printed side facedown so it's not so noticeable. Then I clip the whole thing together with a bulldog clip and write out the title, very cool, Trevor-style.

"What's that?" Michael asks.

"It's my official Kingdom of Fungi Identification Notebook," I say. Ferguson didn't say it had to be an expensive notebook. At least it's something. "Listen to this," I read from my science book. "Mushrooms don't have seeds because they're not plants, and they don't lay eggs or give birth, so what do they do?"

"They die," Michael guesses.

He and Tish are watching the Jell-O box sink.

I pick it up and throw it out. Miraculously, they don't throw a fit. "Here's what mushrooms do," I say to keep their attention away from the boat. "They shoot out spores. Little round things made of super-hard stuff called chitin. Mushrooms shoot out lots of spores, hoping that they'll land in the dirt and start new mushrooms. Listen to this. . . . A scientist measured the force and found that spores can blast off a mushroom with ten thousand times more force than the space shuttle uses to blast out of the Earth's orbit."

Michael blasts water out of the tub.

"Don't make a mess, Little Man, or you'll have to clean it up. Listen to this. . . . Spores are so small they blow away in the wind. Some scientists think maybe spores can fly through space without getting crushed or blown up or fried because they're made of that hard chitin stuff, which means that it might be possible that mushrooms from Earth can travel to other planets."

Michael and Tish laugh even though they have no idea what I'm talking about. After they're done with their baths they run around without any clothes until I make them get dressed. I put Tish in her good dress so that Wayne will see how cute she is.

I stick my head way out the window to see if Wayne is coming. He might have changed a little, but I'll recognize him because he's tall with the longest neck and the smallest head I've ever seen. My nickname for him was Giraffe, which used to always make Mom laugh.

A grandma is walking home with a baby tied to her back. A group of high school girls are waiting at the bus stop. No Giraffe.

Michael comes over and makes me move so he can see if Charlie is still written in the windowsill. He gets me the blue chalk and makes me write all our names over. "Make 'em fresh," he says. Not bad vocabulary for a little man. When he's not looking I write another name. *Wayne.* I focus all my energy into thinking about Wayne and send it out the window, like I'm calling his butt here. *Wayne. Wayne. Wayne.* You never know. Maybe it could work. When I was Michael's age, I used to call for my dad like that. *Dad. Dad. Dad.* Only that was stupid because even if my dad could hear it, he couldn't just walk out of prison.

I look out the window. In the parking lot, Juan is juggling, Markus is riding around and around on that bike he stole, and Microphone Mouth is out sitting on the fence singing like she's got an audience. Diamond's mom comes out and yells at her and Diamond gets up and follows her back to their building.

The bus comes and no Giraffe gets off.

Sometimes I imagine there was some big mistake and my dad got framed and really didn't steal the stuff they said he did. I imagine him getting out and finding me.

Three cars go by. None of them pull in.

Everywhere you look there's another apartment building. Window. Window. Window. Window. Windows stacked on top of windows. People stacked on top of people. Once when I was little, we had a basement apartment and the windows had bars on them. Mom said it was to keep people from breaking in, but I didn't like those bars. That place felt like a jail.

On the bus ride to school, as soon as you cross Branch Road, there aren't any more apartments. And once you get to Buckingham Heights, the houses get big and have nice green grass. I bet Xander and Langley live in those kind of houses. I'd like a house with grass.

Five times there are footsteps in the hallway, but nobody knocks on our door.

Michael and Tish get hungry, so I give them cereal, and Tish spills milk all over her dress. "Momma's gonna be mad," Michael says, which makes Tish cry.

After a while, they go to sleep.

I go back to the window and concentrate as hard as I can. *Wayne. Wayne. Wayne.*

The bus comes and goes three times, and Wayne doesn't get off.

The fourth time the bus comes, my mom gets off.

I watch her walk all the way across the parking lot and past Diamond's building. She doesn't look up once.

I rub the *Wayne* off the windowsill, and then curl

up on my mattress in the living room, pretending to be asleep. I don't want her to ask me if Wayne came. I don't want to see the look on her face when I say no. I picture her walking up to our building and opening the front door. What if Mudman is in the stairwell with the empty bottle in his hand? Even though I'm still mad at my mom, I don't want anything to happen to her. *Shut up*, I say to my heart because it's pounding way too loud. I hold my breath.

I wonder how loud a baby's heart beats. Could Charlie hear his own heart beating in the Dumpster? Did it echo?

Babies should be made out of chitin—that hard stuff that mushroom spores are made of—so no matter what happens they'll be okay.

She must be walking up the stairs real slow because it takes forever before I hear footsteps in the hallway.

I close my eyes and try to quiet down my heart. First come the sounds—the lock turning, shoes being kicked off, the backpack plopping on the kitchen table, bare footsteps on the floor. Then the air around me shifts and she's there, bending down. She smells like sweat and French fries, and those smells make me sadder than I already am. I want to open my eyes and tell her about Langley and Xander and the team and how I need to go to tryouts tomorrow. I want to tell her about my Kingdom of Fungi Identification Notebook and how I want to do good in that class. I want to ask her if my dad has ever asked about me. I want to ask her if she thinks Wayne will come later tonight and slip the money under the door while we're asleep. But my throat is closed like my eyes.

I feel her move away.

When she leaves, the air over me gets heavy, like there is a cement slab coming down on me and there's no way I can push through it. I lay perfectly still. When there aren't any more sounds coming from the bedroom, I get up. It's just hard to sleep sometimes.

GANODERMA APPLANATUM. Common name: ARTIST CONK

Some mushrooms don't look like what I think of when I think of mushrooms. This is a flat "shelf mushroom" that recycles dead trees. Releases 30 billion spores a day! One of the biggest mushrooms in the world. It's nicknamed artist conk because you can actually make drawings on it. When you press down on the surface with a tool, like a sharp stick, the pores stain brown, like ink bleeding up.

Mr. Ferguson said there were fungi before plants and animals on land 1.3 billion years ago.

PSST, HEY GRANDPA?

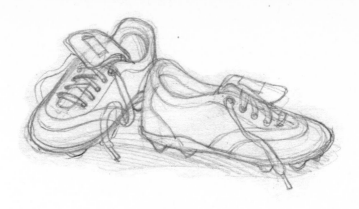

13.
DECISIONS

"Did he come?" It's the first thing out of my mouth when I wake up. Mom is in the bathroom, and she knows right away what I'm talking about.

"No," she calls out.

I lay back down and let it sink in. No Wayne. No money.

Michael runs in and hits me.

"Ow. What's that for?"

"You said if I got clean, something good might happen. But I went to sleep and there's no new backpack. All we got is a new baby."

My mom walks in with a huge baby in her arms, a fat baby boy with yellow snot coming out of his nose.

"Don't tell me he was the free prize that came in the cereal box."

She laughs and wipes his nose. "I got me my first day-care business. He just got dropped off."

Michael takes his thumb out of his mouth. "His name is Rex like a T. rex."

Tish bangs Mom on the leg. "Me up. Me up."

"Ow!" Mom squats down so Tish can see. More snot comes out of the baby's nose.

"Honey, it's just snot," Mom says, wiping it away again. "Why do you have to be so interested in snot?"

"That's what happens when you don't have a TV," I say. "Your children want to watch snot coming out of a T. rex nose."

Mom laughs. "I'm babysitting him until four thirty every day of the week. And his mom says maybe she knows another woman with twins who needs a sitter. And last night I got a part-time job at the Fry Factory. It's from five to ten. . . . You're going to have to watch your brother and sister, so make sure you come home by four forty-five. You don't have to watch Rex, but you do have to watch—"

My slave radar alarm goes off. "No. No. No. No. No."

"What do you mean no?"

"I mean I can't babysit today." Today is tryout day.

"Trev, I don't think you realize how serious this is. It's called rent."

"Why can't you just get one good job? Why do you need two?"

"If I get a job during the day, I have to pay for day care for Tish. That's what happened with that job at the store. Day care ate my whole paycheck. That's why I'm trying to put together my own day-care business." She hoists T. rex over her shoulder and he thanks her by shooting a stream of perfectly white vomit right down her back.

Tish and Michael squeal.

"What happened?" Mom asks, and then she feels it sink in.

"Great," I say. "We got us a Super Soaker."

When she takes Rex into the bathroom, I have a moment to consider what this new night job means to me. School gets out at three. She said that I need to be back at four forty-five, which means that if I hurry, I think I could try out and be back in time.

Now, if I tell her what I'm doing, she's just going to worry that I'll be late, so I figure I'll save her the stress. If there's one thing I know, my mom doesn't need any more stress right now.

When she's not looking, I slip the shin guards and cleats into my backpack. I want to wear a nice jersey and new shorts, but I don't have anything nice. I don't even have anything clean.

The minute I leave the apartment my stomach gets all nervous. What if I mess up? What if I don't make a single goal, or worse, a single decent pass? Or what if Xander's still mad?

In between first- and second-period classes, Matt Salani asks for a shoe creation with his name. I want to keep my business going to cover whatever fees the soccer team might charge, so I say yes, but I'm so worried about tryouts I almost turn his last name into Salami.

I'm dreading lunch because I'm not sure how things are going to be between me and Xander, but Langley sees me as I'm walking in and says, "Hey, Musgrove!" He's obviously glad to see me, and Xander seems okay, too, although he calls me Mushroom again. Today he's wearing a T-shirt with a soccer ball on it and a slogan: IF AT FIRST YOU DON'T SUCCEED, IT'S BECAUSE OF ME.

I set down my tray, racking my brain for something to say when Langley borrows my spoon, blows on it, and hangs it on the end of his nose. It's the kind of thing you do when you're seven, but Langley makes it funny.

I throw a French fry at him. It hits the spoon, which goes flying across the table, and lands—no lie—in Ben's pudding cup. Everybody laughs.

We spend the rest of the lunch period setting up targets, and Xander is in on it, which is cool.

Langley is great. He tells me that The Plague is going to watch the DC United game on Friday night, so if I make the team I should come, which would be sweet.

After lunch when I stop at my locker, Xander catches up with me on his own. He asks me which teachers I've got for each class, all casual. And then he asks how come I'm only in Summit science and he tells me how Summit history and English are so much better than the regular classes. "If you're in Summit science, you should probably be in those," he says. I'm not sure how to read it. Is he saying he wants me to be in his classes or that there must be something wrong with me if I'm not?

I pull out the book I need and he sees the cleats.

"Are those your cleats?" he asks.

"No. They're my grandma's."

He laughs and starts walking away. "Hey," he calls back. "A bunch of other really good kids are trying out today. Are you still planning on coming?"

I close my locker door. "Yep," I say.

"Cool. Good luck!" He walks away.

He *said* good luck, so how come I'm not sure if he meant it?

During English, I finish my work early and crack open my science book to get a jump on my homework. Mr. Ferguson is the first teacher who has ever given homework that I actually don't mind doing.

TUBER MELANOSPORUM
Common name:
PERIGORD BLACK TRUFFLE

Winner of the Most Expensive Food Award. Some people pay $500 - $1500 for one pound of this famous mushroom. It's hard for people to find, but not for pigs. So people use pigs to sniff them out. Or dogs. Mr. Ferguson said dogs are better because they don't eat the truffles. Ever wrestle a pig for a truffle? Don't try, he said!

TRUFFLE PIE, MONSIEUR.

I wonder who was the first person to think of eating this thing? I also wonder what it tastes like?
If they are worth that much, why don't more people have mushroom farms? Maybe I'll have a mushroom farm when I grow up.

I think it's very cool that something most people think is garbage can be worth so much cash.

14.
McCLOUD AND MUSGROVE

Next class is science. Xander acts all buddy-buddy when Langley is around, but I can feel this tension coming from him. I don't think it's my imagination. Sometimes my mom says, "I'm stuck between a rock and a hard place," and I never really understood what she meant until now. I'm stuck between a rock and a hard place with The Plague. If I try out for the team and don't make it, I'll be humiliated. But if I make it, I have this feeling that Xander will hate me. So what am I supposed to do?

"Ladies and Gentlemen, get out your Identification Notebooks, and do not get comfortable," Mr. Ferguson says, putting his Irish cap on his little white Afro. "We shall be perambulating to the front of the school to embark upon an experiment in physics!" He pauses and steps toward me. "Will I be happily surprised today, Mr. Musgrove?"

I get out my homemade, bulldog-clipped Identification Notebook, and Xander laughs at it like *What garbage bag did you find that in?*

Mr. Ferguson nods. "That will suffice."

"Um—if we're doing physics are we done with fungi?" Mosquito Boy asks.

"Not in the slightest. David and Sam, please grab that bin of books. Come along. You'll see."

Off he goes.

"Perambulate this way," Langley says, and does another funny walk.

I push Xander out of my mind and clown around with Langley on the way.

Mr. Ferguson taps the sidewalk with his walking stick. "Who would like to try lifting this piece of concrete?"

"Um, without any equipment?" Mosquito Boy asks. "That's impossible."

Langley goes into his bodybuilding routine again, which makes everybody laugh.

"Impossible for humans, perhaps," Mr. Ferguson says. "But here's a true story. In Russia, the sidewalks all around a large museum started to rise up. People wondered what was happening . . . gases from beneath the earth pushing up? Or some huge burrowing creature? And then some brave individuals worked up the courage to peek under the concrete, and what do you think they saw?"

I guess, "A giant mushroom."

"Close, Mr. Musgrove! Not one giant mushroom, but ordinary little white—what we call button—mushrooms. The same kind you get in your grocery store. The building had been built on the grounds of an old horse stable, and so the earth underneath was rich with horse manure."

"That is so gross," Lydia says.

"Not if you're a mushroom! Mushrooms are coprophilic. Who recalls reading what that means?"

Mosquito Boy raises his hand. "Coprophilic

means having an affection for manure."

Mr. Ferguson laughs. "Affection! Wonderful word choice!"

"That's my new insult," Langley says. "You are so coprophilic!"

Mosquito Boy begins to argue with Mr. Ferguson about whether or not the story is true.

"Mushrooms are deceptively strong." Mr. Ferguson makes a fist and pushes it up. "Hydraulic power. A mushroom called the shaggy mane has been known to break through asphalt and sometimes cement." He shows us a photo and gives us a few more facts about the *Coprinus comatus*. And then he says, "Mr. Musgrove, are you paying attention?"

I show him my notes, and he nods his approval.

"Okay. Now it's your turn. We're going to do a little book research. And since the temperature is so delightful, I thought we could work out of doors."

I love this guy.

He takes us to the back of the school again, where there's grass and trees, and tells us to split into pairs and look through one of his mushroom books together. "Find a mushroom or fungi that you both agree is *interesting*. Make an entry for it in your Identification Notebooks and plan an *interesting* way to present your facts to the whole group—don't just go like this." He pretends to read a paragraph straight from a book. "Boring! You know what I mean? See how I used the concrete to illustrate how mushrooms are strong? Find a way to illustrate your fact. And mix it up. Work with someone other than your lab table partner."

"Come on, Musgrove," Langley says. "Let's do this thing."

I don't even look at Xander, but I can tell he's

pissed, like there's a law against Langley and me being friends.

Langley and I find a big tree to sit under. He cracks open the *Field Guide to Mushrooms*. "Which one should we pick? Listen to the names of some of these mushrooms: stinkhorn, puffball, hen of the woods, death cap, dead man's fingers, witch's butter, turkey tail . . ."

"I bet that's what Mr. Ferguson named his kids," I say. "Come here, little turkey tail, I have to change your diaper!"

Langley laughs and points out a picture of a shiitake mushroom. "My dad loves these things. They smell disgusting."

"Let's do the presentation like a news thing." I grab a stick and pretend it's a microphone. "Trev Musgrove, reporting live." I pick up a pinecone and hold it up like a prop. "This is a stinkhorn mushroom. Fact: It is butt ugly. My analysis is that people should pay us to eat it. And now, back to you in the studio, Langley."

"We should find something uglier for you to hold up."

"A dog turd!" I start looking around for one, and we both crack up.

"Okay, here's a good one." He reads: "'The *Amanita virosa*, otherwise known as the destroying angel, is a beautiful white mushroom, bearing a similar appearance to the white button mushroom commonly found in grocery stores. However, the destroying angel is deadly, containing a poison called amatoxin. Unfortunately symptoms don't appear for five to twenty-four hours, after which time the toxins may have already damaged the liver and kidneys. The symptoms include vomiting, cramps, delirium, convulsions, and diarrhea.'"

The list strikes us both as funny. "I can see why Ferguson loves these things."

Langley goes on. "'As little as half a cap can result in death.'" He grabs the stick. "This is Langley McCloud in the studio. We are about to go live to Washington Hospital, where Dr. Mushroom McMusgrove has just completed a study on the deadly poisonous mushroom known as the destroying angel. Dr. McMusgrove, can you tell us the results?"

I take the stick. "Well, Langley, I have made an important discovery."

"What's that, Doctor?"

"All my patients died."

We plump up our routine with some fine fungal facts and practice it again. When we do it for everybody, the whole class laughs and Mr. Ferguson gives us an A on the spot.

Xander's presentation with a kid named Nicolas would put a corpse to sleep and Xander knows it. As Nicolas drones on, Xander's face keeps getting redder and redder, like he's in the process of swallowing the *Amanita embarrassia* mushroom.

After class as we're walking in, he mutters to Langley, "I'm never working with Nicolas again. I don't know how he got into this program."

"You should've picked Stephanie," Langley says. "Hers rocked."

"Hers was idiotic."

"Well, ours was the best," Langley says. "*Amanita virosa*. You eat. You die." He goes into a slow-motion death sequence, grabbing all the girls on the way in.

"Give him mouth-to-mouth!" I yell out, and all the girls start screaming and laughing and pushing him away.

- AMANITA VIROSA -
Common name: The Destroying Angel

YOU EAT, YOU DIE!

This is why Mr. Ferguson says you should NOT eat mushrooms that you find in the wild unless someone like a mycologist has identified them.

... it can grow into a whole new fungus.

If a piece of mycelium is broken off... and moved

15.
TRYOUTS

Here's my plan. Just mind my own business. Go to tryouts and do my best.

In P.E., I'm not in either Xander's or Langley's group, which is good. I focus on trying to stay positive and loose.

"You trying out for the Toilers?" Juan asks.

When I tell him I'm trying out for an MCS Elite team after school, I can tell he's impressed.

"Second place last year in Division One," I say. "They need a striker to get to first place."

"Lucky," Juan says. "You're solid. You're going to make it."

I take that in and hold on to it. I can do this thing if I don't tense up.

Langley catches me at dismissal and invites me to walk with them. Like I said, around Langley, Xander is okay. He whips out his cell phone and texts Ben while we're walking. Three blocks from the school, Langley heads up a driveway to the biggest house on the street. "Let's stop and get something to drink," he says.

A Merry Maids van is parked in front. The front lawn is perfect. A big yard of green grass. The door isn't locked, so we just walk in. Two women are just leaving, loaded with cleaning supplies.

"Perfect timing," Langley says.

The whole house feels refrigerated and smells like lemons. It's more like a picture of a house than a real house. There is a piano and pictures in silver frames on it. Something smelling like roast beef is cooking, and my stomach wants to scream.

"It's me and Xander," Langley calls out. "And somebody new."

"Take off your shoes," a voice calls back.

"Everything was just cleaned."

The carpeting is smooshy and soft and white, and I glance back, hoping not to see any dirty footprints coming from me.

Through large glass doors, I can see the backyard, complete with a tree house and soccer goals and balls everywhere.

We walk into the kitchen, and his mom is there at a computer, typing really fast. She's got red wavy hair, just like Langley. "Eat something healthful," she says without looking up. Then she realizes that she hasn't met me so she stops and introduces herself and tells me to make myself at home and then she goes back to her work. The refrigerator is huge and metallic with ice-water delivery right from the door. Langley flings open a closet, revealing shelves and shelves, full of food. Like a grocery store.

"What do you want?" Langley asks.

I don't know what I should say. I want everything. Before I can pick, a little red-haired girl runs in and punches Langley on the side just as he is taking a long drink.

"Hey, that hurt, you coprophilic fungus!" Langley

wipes the water off his chin and grabs her in a headlock.

"What'd you call me?" the girl asks.

"A manure-loving mushroom."

"Yuck."

"Her name is Emma," the mom calls out.

"Hey, our teacher said moms are like fungi," Langley says.

Before his mom can respond, footsteps come down the stairs behind them and Emma starts to squeal. A man's voice booms: "Fee, Fi, Fo, Foy. I smell the blood of a girl and boy."

Langley rolls his eyes. "He does this every day."

The door opens and Langley's dad walks in. He is tall and has this square chin and looks like a guy on a shaving commercial. "I knew I smelled children!" he says, scooping up Emma and flipping her upside down. "Hey, Langley. Hey, Xander. Ah, this must be the soccer player."

Langley introduces me, and his dad says that he'll watch tryouts because he needs a break from work.

My mom always says that just because you've

got a nice house doesn't mean you've got a nice family. Langley has both.

Langley grabs a bag with his cleats and shin guards and fills up water bottles for me, Xander, and himself. His dad leads the way. I haven't taken anything from the closet and now it's too late. I am so hungry I feel like taking a bite out of the door on the way out.

Buckingham Park is five blocks away—it's a big park with a soccer field, a playground for little kids, and even a pool. Xander and Langley are talking about the team and arguing about who has the best skills, and I'm giving myself an internal pep talk when I notice the mushrooms. Three of them. Crazy big. Each one is tall with a perfect domed cap about the size of a cantaloupe that's been cut in half. They're bizarre and magical-looking, like maybe they're homes for little elves or fairies.

Mr. Ferguson said that we'd start to notice mushrooms in unexpected places, and he was right.

"Guess what," I say. "We're perambulating toward some fungi!"

Xander and Langley both look up. I'm perambulating faster so I can take a closer look, but then Xander takes a few jogging steps forward and kicks the cap off each one. *Bam. Bam. Bam.*

"I'm telling Mr. Fungus on you," Langley says.

There's two more mushrooms farther ahead, and I'm imagining the little elves inside gearing up to try and defend themselves from the Evil Destroyer, but Xander kicks them to pieces, too.

I know they're just mushrooms, but the wreckage makes me sad.

My mom says I came home once from Head Start all excited because I got a book of nursery rhymes that I was allowed to keep, but when she read the one about how nobody could put Humpty Dumpty back together, I got so upset I wouldn't look at the book again.

What can I say? I'm a sensitive guy.

"Let the games begin!" Xander calls out to a bunch of guys. They are sitting on a grassy slope, putting on their cleats, none of them familiar from school. They all start joking with Xander and Langley. I sit down to gear up. Everybody has matching red Nike backpacks and matching soccer socks. I don't have soccer socks, which is embarrassing, and the cleats are much tighter than they were in the store.

Xander is showing off his new cleats. The coach—long dark hair in a ponytail—is talking to other parents who are introducing the kids who are trying out, asking what teams their kids were on last year. Langley's dad waits until the coach is done talking to the other parents, then he introduces me.

The sun feels like a spotlight, so hot I could burst into flames.

"What position do you play, lad?" Coach Evan asks. I like his British accent.

I remember Langley saying that they needed a striker, so I say, "Striker."

"What team did you play on last season?"

I tell him that I moved around last year, and he drops it.

As he puts us through warm-ups and drills, I try to focus on whatever I have to do so that I won't think about how nervous I am and how much the cleats are already hurting my feet. Then he splits us into teams for a scrimmage.

I'm assigned to be a striker on Xander's team. Langley is playing the same position for the opposing team.

As soon as the ball is in, Xander is all over the field. Every time he gets the ball, he tries to score on his own.

"I'm open," I shout, but Xander won't pass.

I try not to get angry, try to stay focused and ready in case the ball comes my way. *Come on, Xander. Play fair.*

Xander scores twice.

My feet begin to blister.

The coach blows the whistle and changes the positions of several players. He switches me over to the team Langley is on and asks him to play midfielder.

It's 2–0, Xander's team. I start with the ball for my new team. I pass it to one of our other guys. Xander steals it and tries to run for the goal, faking out two players along the way. Xander is about to make another move, but Langley steals it, passes the ball to me, and I'm dead center mid-field. I make a turn with the ball and head to the goal. I see my chance and take a shot. The keeper dives, but it hits the post and it ricochets in. 2–1.

Xander's team starts with the ball. Their forward passes it back and they have possession.

A minute later Langley gets the ball again and makes a crisp pass to our right wing. The winger tries to make a pass, but Xander is right there to intercept. I go shoulder to shoulder and push him off the ball.

"Foul!" Xander cries. "He totally elbowed me."

"I'll make the calls," Coach Evan says. "Keep playing."

I pass the ball.

"It was a foul." Xander won't let it go. He's not even going for the ball. It's like he wants to start World War III.

The striker on Xander's team calls out, "Xander, keep playing."

Langley makes this funny face and whispers to me, "I don't know what's biting his butt."

We split up. I make a run and Langley sends a

through ball. I run past the last defender and now it's just me and the goalie. I pull the ball sharply to the left and lose the keeper. It is a clear-cut path to glory. I'm about to get my second goal.

Langley calls out, "Man on!"

Before I can react, someone slams into my ankles from behind and I'm down.

The whistle blows.

"PK," the coach calls out. "Clearly from behind, Xander. I never want to see that again. If this were a game, you'd be out."

"He tripped! I didn't do anything—"

The coach squats by me. "Lad? Eh? All in one piece?"

Langley's dad appears.

I'm not sure what hurts more. My ankle, the hip I landed on, or the fact that Xander slide-tackled me.

"Do we have a parent's cell phone?" Coach Evan is asking Langley's dad.

I sit up. "I'm okay." Specks of light dance around my head, and I think I might throw up. *You're okay*, I tell myself.

The coach gives me a hand, and when I stand up, the rawness of my blistered feet slices through all the rest of the pain. "Walk it off, Trev, is it? Walk it off. Xander, over here for a minute." The coach asks Langley's dad to join them and he pulls Xander over to the side. I can hear bits and pieces of the lecture.

"No, Xander. It's your temper. That's what happened at the end of our last game, remember? I won't tolerate it. As you can see, there are other lads who would like a chance to be on the team. I'm going to talk to your dad about it one more time. Sit out for the rest of this scrimmage and think about it."

The coach blows the whistle and gives the ball to me for the penalty kick.

Xander's hatred for me streams from the sideline. My head aches. The pain from my feet shoots up my legs.

I run up to the ball, hesitate to throw off the keeper, and nail it. The ball flies over the goalie's head and into the goal.

"Brilliant shot," Coach Evan says. "Right in the upper ninety."

Langley slaps me on the back. "McBrilliant, Musgrove!"

The coach rearranges positions and tries me on defense for another short game. Just when I think I might drop dead, he announces laps and everybody groans. No problem, I think, just let me take my feet off first. It's going to kill me and make me late—but I run the laps. I'm worried that the coach won't take me seriously if I leave early.

Langley makes it fun by impersonating teachers whenever Coach Evan isn't watching. He tucks his head down so he has no neck and he runs like a refrigerator. "Okay, people!" he says. "Let's get going." He looks just like Coach Stevins. The funniest is when he pretends to hold a walking stick and runs with short, squatty steps. "Let us perambulate to the egress for a foray," he says in a perfect imitation of Mr. Ferguson's voice.

When Coach Evan dismisses the team, he asks me to stay for a minute. Xander takes off. The coach tells the parents of the other kids who were trying out that he'll e-mail them with a decision. Then he has a one-on-one hushed conversation with Langley's dad, and I can tell they're talking about me.

"Plug your nose. My shoes are coming off." Langley sits down next to me and unties his cleats. "By the way . . . Xander sometimes gets out of control."

"Yeah. I sort of picked up on that."

"He just really, really, really wants to win."

"Really?" I take off my cleats and peel off my bloody socks.

"Call 911, man," Langley says. "Cover them up! I can't stand the sight of blood."

I pour water onto my feet and wince. Then Coach Evan motions for me to come over.

"Well, lad," he says. "You were offsides twice. A couple of your runs were a bit wild, and you need a wider field of vision. You've got to watch the whole field, not just the ball . . . but . . ." He smiles. "You're very hungry."

"I didn't get too much lunch—"

He laughs. "I mean hungry for the ball. That's what I want in a player. You're fast and you've got a strong kicking leg and you're hungry for that ball. You go for it and you don't stop until you've got it and then you see it through to the goal or you pass it. . . . You're a good team player. We'll need to talk to your parents. But we'd like to invite you on the team."

Langley's dad smiles and pats me on the back. "What's your dad's e-mail address? I'll send him all the information about the team."

I can hardly think straight. I mumble something about how my dad is on a business trip and our computer has been down. They ask me to put my name, address, and phone number on a form, which is a problem because I don't really want them knowing I'm from Deadly Gardens and I don't want them calling Mom yet because I haven't figured out how to talk her into saying yes. So I ask them if I can take it home with me and return it later. Langley's dad takes a card out of his wallet and hands it to me. "Well, have your mom or dad give me a call tonight or tomorrow morning at the latest."

The coach notices my feet. "Crikey! What happened?"

"My cleats are a little tight."

"A little? If you played that well with blisters, I'd like to see how well you play without. Bandage those up and get your mum or dad to take you out for new cleats before Friday. Right then?"

"Sure," I say. "No problem."

16.
CELEBRATE

When I walk in the door, Michael takes his thumb out of his mouth and says with big eyes, "Momma's real mad at you, Trev. You're late."

Tish is walking around in circles, holding on to a full roll of toilet paper and letting a little drag out behind her like she's a one-girl parade.

I lean against the door to catch my breath as Mom steps out of the bathroom. She is wearing ugly brown pants and a brown shirt that says FRY FACTORY. The underarms of her shirt are wet.

I'm afraid she'll yell and shout. Instead she won't even look at me. She grabs her backpack.

I try to apologize, but she snaps, "I will be back

at ten thirty or so. It's the Fry Factory on Eighth Street. The number is on the table." She hands me her cell phone. "Call and ask for me only if there's an emergency. Do *not* leave this apartment." The door slams. Then she bangs on it. "Lock this right now."

I lock it. And she's gone.

Michael and Tish stare at me. I'm still out of breath.

I pick up Tish and twirl around. "I made the team!" I grab the toilet paper roll, throw it into the air, and catch it again.

Tish doesn't know what I'm talking about. She just wants her toy back. *"Mine!"* she yells, reaching for the roll.

"That's right! *Yours!*" I laugh and hand the roll back to Tish.

She tries to throw the toilet paper in the air except it hits me in the head.

"Oh! You got me!" I collapse and tackle her. She squeals, and Michael jumps on my back. I throw the roll in the air and it unspools, covering us with a long white ribbon.

PLEUROTUS OSTREATUS

common name:

OYSTER MUSHROOM

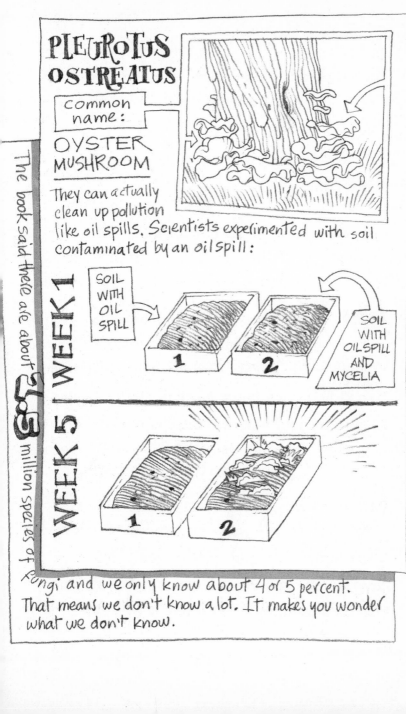

They can actually clean up pollution like oil spills. Scientists experimented with soil contaminated by an oil spill:

WEEK 1

SOIL WITH OIL SPILL

1

2

SOIL WITH OIL SPILL AND MYCELIA

WEEK 5

1

2

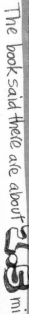

fungi and we only know about 4 or 5 percent. That means we don't know a lot. It makes you wonder what we don't know.

17.
XANDER

Last night I did my homework and went to bed early so I wouldn't have to tell Mom why I didn't come home after school. This morning, I can't bring up the subject of soccer or ask her to fill out the form, because it's like I'm living in a toxic oil spill. Mom is going crazy because Michael is refusing to go to school without a new backpack. He wet the bed in the middle of the night, and we all woke up late, and I barely had enough time to grab clothes out of the pile of dirty laundry and throw them on. Then, of course, T. rex, the little King of Snotland, shows up.

On the bus Juan says, "Sorry, man."

"About what?"

"You didn't make the team?"

"I made it."

"How come you don't look happy?"

I tell him it's complicated.

I have two problems, as I see it. My mom. And Xander. I need a plan for each. Badly. I keep to myself on the bus and try to think things through. Mom first. What if I tell her the truth? Will she let me be on the team? About as likely as her buying me a cell phone for my birthday. What if I spruce up the truth a little and tell her that I have to stay after school twice a week for . . . homework help? What if I convince the coach to let me run home rather than do laps . . . then would I get home in time for her to go to the Fry Factory? I think that's my best bet.

Then there's Xander. The best solution to that problem would be for him to disappear, but that is not going to happen. I think I have to mind my own business. If I end up helping to take The Plague to the top, maybe he'll end up liking me.

Just as I'm opening my locker door, Diamond

runs over, dragging Celine along with her. "Look." She shows the pictures in my locker door to Celine before I have the chance to close it. "He's gonna be a famous artist," she says to Celine, and then she rips a piece of paper out of her notebook. "Do my name, my logo, and sign it—"

"You can sell it on eBay," Celine says.

"No," Diamond says. "I'm gonna save it and use it for my first album cover."

I put her paper on top of my binder and write LEAVE ME ALONE. I sign it and hand it back.

Xander is walking down the hall toward me, so I turn my back on them and open my door again.

Celine reads my message out loud and says, "Oooh, he's playing hard to get, Diamond."

"Shut up." Diamond hits Celine. Then she says, "Well, I got your signature anyway, so maybe I will sell it on eBay. Ha-ha."

Celine goes to class, but Diamond wouldn't get a hint if you hit her over the head with it, so she just hangs there like she has the right to.

Xander walks by and says under his breath, "I thought only girls decorated their lockers."

He lets it fly like an arrow dipped in poison.

I put up my shield and let it bounce off me.

But Diamond starts having a fit and calling Xander names.

"Sorry, Mushroom," Xander calls back. "Since you've got a girlfriend I guess that means you're not gay, but you smell like you peed your pants."

I can't move. My brain hurts. My feet hurt. My feelings hurt. My whole life hurts. I pulled my clothes from the dirty pile this morning. They do smell like pee.

I wish my locker worked like that magic closet in that movie. I wish I could just step right inside it and keep walking into another world. Or maybe I could shrink and go live in a giant mushroom.

In Computer Applications, I get yelled at for doodling while Ms. Cho is talking. I keep trying to explain that drawing helps me pay attention, but Ms. Cho doesn't pay attention when I'm talking to her. It isn't fair. My new daydream is to push the delete button and watch the entire class disappear.

To avoid passing by Xander's locker, I take a different route to my next class and pass by the art room. I love the smell of art rooms. They're big and full and the air smells like color. Wish I had art instead of Computer Applications.

In U.S. History, we take turns reading about the Great Depression and a guy named Sean falls asleep with his mouth open and my finger is itching to flick a spitwad in it, but I can't afford to get in any trouble, so I keep my little fingers to myself like a good American citizen.

Math = yawn x yawn (+ yawn) x 100yawn[10]

After math, Diamond passes a note to me in the hallway.

RU gonna get Xander?

I throw it away.

School is the Great Depression.

18.
FRAMED

I'm dreading lunch and wishing I didn't have to go, and then—lucky me—Xander comes along and shoves me up against a locker before I get there.

"I know you wrote it, Musgrove."

"Wrote what?"

"The stuff on my locker."

"What stuff?"

"What seems to be the problem, boys?" It's Ms. Ramone, the same teacher who took away my permanent marker on the first day of school.

Next thing I know I'm in the vice principal's

office. Somebody wrote "profanity" on Xander's locker with a permanent marker, and I'm being blamed for it.

I'm mad, but it doesn't pay to blow up. I push my anger down and focus on staying calm. This is my first time meeting Mr. Gonzalez, and I want to make a good impression. Getting in trouble is bad enough, but getting in trouble for something you didn't do is just ridiculous.

"Mr. Gonzalez, I didn't vandalize Xander's locker." I add a little smile because innocent people have something to smile about and guilty people never do.

Mr. Gonzalez frowns, leans back, taps his pencil on the arm of his chair, and stares at me like I'm a death cap mushroom that just popped up on his lawn. "Well, Ms. Ramone says that she caught you trying to deface a locker on the first day of school."

Hard to keep smiling.

"I was only *thinking* about it, I didn't *do* it."

"I hear that you have a graffiti business and that you were upset with Xander because he didn't purchase a design from you."

"What? That's not true!" My brain hurts, like I just got kicked in the head. *Stay calm,* I tell myself. *You're innocent. You're innocent.*

"Are you saying that you don't have a graffiti business?"

Why did I have to be such a brilliant entrepreneur? I look him right in the eye. "Mr. Gonzalez. I don't have a graffiti business. I drew a few designs on shoes. Just on shoes. To earn a few bucks." I show him the *Musgrove* on my shoe. "I was not upset with Xander for not buying a design. I did *not* vandalize anything."

Our eyes are locked together. *Please believe me.*

He sighs. "At this point, we have no proof that you did it. Regardless of that, let me say this: You are not allowed to sell or produce any more graffiti on school grounds—even if it's only on shoes. We can't have kids buying and selling stuff because it's disruptive to the learning environment. Is that understood?"

Understood. The bell rings. I missed lunch completely. Does Gonzalez care? No.

I slip through the door, barely alive.

Diamond is hanging right outside the office door. "How come you was in there?" she asks. She sounds scared that I might have gotten in trouble, which makes me suspicious. It's like she has some stake in it. I think back to the note she slipped me—*RU gonna get Xander?* Did she decide to get him for me by writing on his locker?

"Come on," she says. "Celine told me she saw Ramone bringing you in. How come?"

"Maybe you know."

"What do you mean?" Her face goes hard.

"I got called in because somebody wrote on Xander's locker."

"Who do they think did it?"

"Me!"

"They can't blame you. They don't have any proof."

"How do you know I didn't do it?"

Celine comes along and pulls her off to class.

I want to make a label for her.

The thing that I hate about school is that there's no time to stop and think. It doesn't matter if somebody kicks your head off. You just have to pick it up and stick it back on and go from class to class to class to class.

WARNING! THIS GIRL MUST BE HAZARDOUS TO YOUR HEALTH

I've already been late twice to English because it's the class that takes me the longest to get to and I don't want to add a detention to my list, so I hustle. Just before the bell is about to ring, a tug on my binder catches me off guard. I drop everything—books, binder, papers spill out.

It's Xander.

He slips into the doorway of his next class.

19.
FROSTY POD ROT

I'm the last one into Mr. Ferguson's room. I've been dreading this. I'm afraid to see Langley because he probably thinks I wrote on Xander's locker. And I'm afraid to see Xander because I'm going to want to kick him in the face for making me late to English.

"Delighted you decided to join us, Mr. Musgrove," Mr. Ferguson says. "Looks like we're all here." He picks up the big cookie jar shaped like a mushroom.

Xander smiles at me. "Hey, Mushroom, how's it going?"

"Great." I smile back. "I got a detention for being late to English."

He shakes his head. "Better not make that a habit."

Mr. Ferguson walks over. "For your warm-up today, I want each of you to draw a slip of paper out of this cookie jar. On it you will find your fungus of the day. Use the classroom library to make an entry about it in your Identification Notebook and look around the room. Most likely you will be able to locate your fungus, either on a poster up here or in an article on one of the bulletin boards or in real form or in my dried collection on the back shelf."

Everybody chooses a fungus name and gets busy.

As Langley gets up he hands me a piece of paper out of his notebook. "Here's The Plague membership info. My dad said your computer was down and he thought it would be good for you to have."

"Oh, didn't you tell him?" Xander looks at me and then says to Langley, "Musgrove's dad said he can't play on the team."

"Really?" Langley asks.

Xander shrugs. "Am I right, Musgrove?"

I stare Xander down. "Actually, my dad really wants me to be on The Plague."

"Gentlemen," Mr. Ferguson says. "More work, less talk."

Langley walks over to the bookshelf and Xander follows.

I'm going to play on The Plague if it's the last thing I do. There is no way I'm letting Xander win. I can talk the coach into letting me get home on time. I can raise the money somehow, even if I can't sell my designs at school.

Langley and his dad wouldn't give me the membership info if they didn't want me on the team. I unfold The Plague info sheet and the bottom drops out of my stomach.

COST OF TEAM MEMBERSHIP: $1,000.00

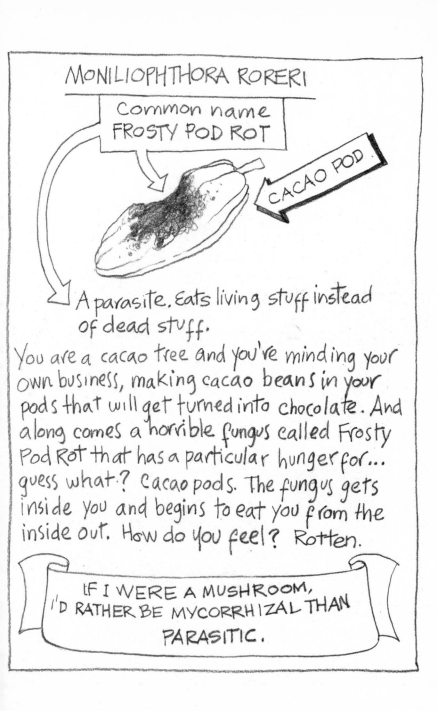

MONILIOPHTHORA RORERI

Common name
FROSTY POD ROT

CACAO POD

A parasite. Eats living stuff instead of dead stuff.

You are a cacao tree and you're minding your own business, making cacao beans in your pods that will get turned into chocolate. And along comes a horrible fungus called Frosty Pod Rot that has a particular hunger for... guess what? Cacao pods. The fungus gets inside you and begins to eat you from the inside out. How do you feel? Rotten.

IF I WERE A MUSHROOM, I'D RATHER BE MYCORRHIZAL THAN PARASITIC.

20.
LOSING IT

There should be a sound when a dream ends. Like a door or a Dumpster lid slamming . . . or something louder . . . a tree splitting . . . or maybe a bomb exploding. Instead, there's no sound at all. Everybody is walking to the next class, and the hallway is filled with noise, but it's sideline noise, and I'm walking, too, dead quiet on the inside. I hate my mom for being right. I can't afford to be on the team. I shouldn't have tried out. I shouldn't have even dreamed about it in the first place.

I get to P.E., and I'm wondering how I'm possibly going to make it through the class when a voice comes over the intercom. "Coach Stevins. Would you please ask Trevor Musgrove to report to the guidance office?"

Guidance? What now?

Stevins dismisses me and I walk down the long silent hallway back to the office, all the lockers standing at attention on either side like a firing squad.

The guidance counselor—Ms. Beitz—looks like she has never smiled in her whole life. "I heard through the grapevine, Trevor, that you're having trouble with your schedule . . . trouble keeping up with your science work, I mean. I checked—"

"I'm keeping up," I say.

She looks at me like if I interrupt again, she'll bite my head off and wash it down with her Diet Coke. She goes on, "What I was about to say was I checked the records and found a computer error in your schedule. You should be in Ms. Becker's science class."

It's guidance counselor code. What she's really saying is that I'm not smart enough to be in a Summit class.

My jaw clenches, and the anger in me rises up. "Who told you I'm having trouble?"

"Is that attitude I detect in your voice?" Ms. Beitz drums her long blue fingernails on her desk. "Because I do not respond well to attitude."

"If Xander Pierce told you, then he is a parasitic fungus."

She sets her pencil down. "What?"

"Oh. Sorry. Only Summit students are supposed to know what big words mean."

Ms. Beitz smolders. "I suggest you ponder what you think you'll gain from disrespecting me."

I crossed her line so fast I'm dizzy.

On the bus ride home, I ponder the hits I've taken. First: I was born. Second: Xander was born. Third: I beat Xander at juggling. Fourth: Diamond was born and rubbed my victory in Xander's face. Fifth: I get blamed for doing graffiti that I didn't even do. Sixth: I get kicked out of the only class I like.

From the back, Markus's voice interrupts my ponder. "What was you thinking would happen, Diamond?"

"Shut up, Mark*ass*," Diamond hisses.

"Hey, Trev," Markus shouts out, "guess what your girlfriend did for you."

"Shut up!" Diamond shouts.

"Sit down, back there!" the bus driver yells. "Next person gets a detention."

I turn around to face them. Diamond looks scared. She tries to cover Markus's mouth, but he pulls her hand away and says, "Diamond defended your honor, man."

I stand up, and the bus driver's voice slams against the back of my head. "I said sit down!"

I'm so mad, I don't care. I walk straight for Diamond. "You did it, didn't you? You did Xander's locker?"

Celine ooohs. "See, I told you he wouldn't like it."

I glare at Diamond. "What part of LEAVE ME ALONE do you not understand?"

The bus has stopped. The bus driver grabs me by the back of my shirt, drags me up to the front of the bus, and forces me into a seat. "You just earned two detentions."

21.
THROWING PUNCHES

I can hear the crying from down the hall. It's Tish. She's lying on the floor, bawling about something. Michael's got his thumb in his mouth and an angry look on his face, and Mom is yelling at him about the backpack he wants. As soon as she sees me she shoots me this hard look with a hundred thousand times more force than mushrooms use to blast their spores. I don't want to go in, but I have nowhere else to go.

"Trev, tell Mom I need a superhero backpack right now," Michael says.

Mom shouts, "Michael, it's over. Case closed.

No backpack. Trev, you've got a lot of explaining to do." She slams the door and makes me sit in a chair. "I called the school today to ask about supplies for you, which is not an easy thing for me to do, you know, and the vice principal, Mr. Gonzalez or something like that, said he called you in because some kid said you wrote on his locker. How many times have I told you—"

"Why is everybody assuming I did it?"

"He said you're already falling behind in Computer Applications and you got a detention for being late. We have a rule that you're supposed to tell me if you get—"

"It's a stupid elective and I'm behind because we don't have a computer for the homework. And you know why I got a detention? Because this guy named Xander has it in for me. He slammed into me and knocked everything down."

"Don't go blaming everybody else."

"Don't go blaming me without knowing what you're talking about."

"I am at the end of my rope, Trev. So don't raise your voice at me."

"I'm defending myself!"

"Nobody is listening to *me*!" Michael screams, and throws himself into the corner.

"Not now, Michael." Mom glares at me. "How many times have I told you that you have to do good in school? It's a brand-new school for you, Trevor; first impressions stick like glue."

"I know!" I throw my backpack against the wall. "I'm trying. You know how hard it is? I have no cell phone. No decent clothes. No shoes. Hey, you want to see this?" I kick off my shoe and pull off my sock and show her my blisters. "See these? I tried out for that team and made it. Did you know that? No. I didn't tell you because I knew you'd just say no. You say no to everything that I want."

"I'm doing the best I can. I spent the day hauling Tish and Rex on the bus over to welfare for a face-to-face. And then I hauled them over to Bestway to get food. And then I hauled everything back here. Four bags and two kids." The more she talks, the madder she gets. "I am trying. I work my butt off for you guys—"

"If you work so hard, how come we never have any money?"

"'Cause you guys are expensive. That's why! It takes money to take care of you. And who's doing it? You don't see your daddy doing it. You don't see their daddy doing it." She points to Michael and Tish. "Who's taking care of you? Me!"

Whoever lives in the apartment next door turns up their music. They're probably the same guys who ripped the picture off our door. "I hate it here. I hate my school. I hate this apartment."

"What am I supposed to do?" Mom yells. "They raised the rent at our old place. We couldn't afford it. Period."

I kick off my other shoe. "Langley's *tree house* is better than this dump."

"Langley, whoever Langley is, was probably born to a family with money."

"How come I wasn't?"

"'Cause you were born to me."

"Well, I wish I wasn't."

That stings. Her eyes are filling up and her face looks hot, like I slapped her. I don't care. I'm too far gone to stop. I'm hungry and tired. All day long I've been kicked by everybody for stuff I didn't even do. I turn my back on her and go into the bedroom. She follows, and I try to shut the door, but she grabs hold of it.

"Who said life is fair, Trev? It ain't. That doesn't mean you can yell at me. That doesn't mean you can mess up at school."

"I hate school. And I hate coming home and babysitting."

"Listen, Trev. You think I *want* to work at the Fry Factory? I'm young. You don't see it, but it's true. I'm young. I'd like to be going out tonight and partying with my friends. Maybe go to a movie. But I can't. I got three kids. I got responsibilities. We gotta do things even when we don't want to. You gotta help out around here, like it or not. And you gotta do good in school. I know you're smart, Trev. I know you can do real good when you have a positive attitude."

"A positive attitude won't make a difference."

"Stop talking like that. You are *not* giving up." Her voice starts shaking like she's going to cry, but she pulls herself together like a statue and doesn't blink. "You think I don't understand, but I do. Right around your age, I started thinking I was just a piece of trash, and I stopped trying.

Who cares about stupid school projects and tests and report cards? There was so much pressure on me I couldn't take it anymore. I know what it's like. But you can't give up like I did! I'm counting on you to do better than me. Once you stop trying, everything else falls apart, Trev. That's what happened to me. All my priorities got messed up. I started partying and messing around with my boyfriend and then I got pregnant and dropped out. Now look at me."

She's standing in the doorway in her Fry Factory uniform. A ray of light from the kitchen is shining on one side of her face. I don't want to look at her right now. Tish is standing behind her, staring at me with wide, scared eyes.

"Momma?" Tish starts to cry again.

"Don't cry. Please," Mom says, and picks up Tish. "It's okay. We're just having a little fight."

Tish calms down right away, and there's something about it that reaches in and punches me in the gut. I'm not a little kid anymore. We're *not* just having a little fight. It's a big fight and it's not okay.

The edges of the room start to get blurry and

my stomach hurts, like maybe I'm going to throw up or faint. "I'm the reason your life is so messed up," I say.

She's just standing there like a statue.

I throw my next sentence at her. "I bet you wished you would've thrown me in the Dumpster when I was born."

BAM!

The apartment is vibrating. I am standing perfectly still, not breathing, just staring at her.

Michael's voice floats up. "Trev is bad," he says.

She's not crumbling, like I thought she would. "Trev, you know that's not true." Her voice comes out thin and cold like she's hollow on the inside. "We have to talk about this, but I can't now. I have to go, and you have to watch Michael and Tish. This is between you and me so don't take it out on them."

I turn my face into stone and stare at her. I'm not crumbling, either.

"If you got homework, you better do it," she says. She gets her stuff together and goes.

I lock the door behind her.

There is exactly two seconds of silence, and then Tish cries, "Momma."

I get milk in a sippy cup and hand it to her to shut her up.

Michael glares at me.

I get leftover hamburgers out. Michael won't eat, so I ignore him and eat mine cold with ketchup.

Tish finally decides to stop crying.

"I'm hungry," Michael says to the wall.

"Nobody's stopping you. Come and eat."

"I'm mad at you. You won't help me and you're mean."

"Then don't eat."

There's a knock on the door.

"Who is it?" I ask without opening it.

"It's Diamond."

I don't move.

"I'm sorry I did that to Xander's locker," she says through the door. "I just come to say that. I thought I was doing you a favor, but I'm sorry."

"Go away."

"Are you gonna tell on me?"

"I don't know."

"Please don't." She's quiet for a few seconds, then she asks if she can come in.

"No," I say.

"Please, Trev."

"Not my problem."

There is a long pause.

"That baby is still at Saint Francis. He's real sick," Diamond says. "He might not make it. I heard it on the news."

Michael takes his thumb out of his mouth. "Charlie?"

I don't say anything.

He runs to the windowsill. "Make his name fresh, Trev."

I want everybody to leave me alone.

"I thought you might want to know," she says.

I don't answer. After a few seconds the sound of her flip-flops echo as she walks down the hall.

BRIDGEOPORUS NOBILISSIMUS

Common name: Noble Polypore

The first mushroom on the endangered species list in North America.
Even though mushrooms produce billions of incredibly tough little spores, I guess you can still wipe out a species.
If you're a mushroom you don't know where you are going to pop up. I guess it's sort of like being human, you don't know where you are going to be born.

22.
IN NEED OF
MAJOR SURGERY

Little Cavewoman wakes me up by sitting on my head.

"Wev," she says, and pinches my nose. "Me stinky diaper."

She ain't kidding.

"Come and sit on the potty, Tish!" Mom says.

"Shouldn't she sit on the potty *before* it all comes out?" Michael asks. He's standing at the window, scratching on the screen with a Popsicle stick.

"Well, I'm just trying to teach her to sit on the potty period. I'm tired of buying diapers. Don't make that hole in the screen bigger, Michael. I just taped it up."

I guess some people wake up to the smell of cinnamon rolls and the sounds of birds chirping. I wake up to this.

"I don't want to go to school," I say.

"I'm not going, either," Michael says.

"You're both going and that's that."

Mom tells me she's calling to make sure I'm in class. She tells me that I have to "inform" The Plague's coach that I can't be on the team. We're both still mad at each other.

Diamond attacks me the minute I show up at the bus stop. "If you told Gonzalez you didn't do it and he believes you, then you're not gonna tell on me, right?"

"He's not the type to turn you in," Celine says.

Markus adds his two cents. "Trevor likes hanging with the Summit boys. He ain't gonna care about saving your butt, Diamond."

The bus pulls up.

I'm going to explode.

"Nobody around here minds their own business," Juan says. "Leave the man alone."

Like I said before, Juan is all right.

I sit next to him on the bus, and he reaches in his pocket and pulls out a piece of candy and gives it to me. Just a little thing, but it kind of saves me for the moment.

Before my first class even starts, I'm called into the office. At this rate they should set aside a special bench in there for me with a little plaque on it: DEDICATED TO TREVOR MUSGROVE, WHO GETS HAULED IN AT LEAST ONCE A DAY.

Mr. Gonzalez hands me the bus driver's report. He explains the two detentions for standing up on the bus, which I'll be serving during lunch, and says that he'll be calling home to let my mom know. By the way, Mr. Gonzalez says, Ms. Beitz informed him about the computer error in my schedule of classes, and now my schedule has been corrected. I'll be in Ms. Becker's class for science.

"But I like Mr. Ferguson's class."

"The only way you can be in a Summit class is to have applied and been accepted into the Summit program," he says.

I can tell by the look on his face that it won't do me any good to argue.

No more perambulating outside. No more Irish caps and walking sticks. No more fungi facts and mycelium demonstrations.

I sleepwalk through the morning and serve detention during lunch.

Diamond tries to talk to me on my way to English. "I got an idea of how I can make up for what I did," she says. "I'm gonna get you something you're really gonna like."

"Try dying instead," I say. "That might do the trick."

I'm not a mean person, but sometimes I just can't take it anymore.

In English, I get yelled at again for doodling.

In my new science class, we spend the entire period reading out of the textbook and I swear the place smells like an old lunch sack. Since there is absolutely nothing in the classroom except Ms. Becker, my excellent supposition is that the stink is her perfume. Eau de Tuna Fish and Rotten Bananas. Markus is in that class, and every time the teacher isn't looking, he fires a spitwad at the ceiling. He's like a giant *Ganoderma applanatum* shooting out spores. He's got a billion spitwads up there.

I spend the entire period either trying not to: a) smell Ms. Becker; b) think about what Mr. Ferguson is doing; or c) obsess about Xander.

Just before the bell rings, the office calls on the intercom.

"Ms. Becker, do you have Trevor Musgrove?"

"Yes."

Everybody goes "ooh" like I'm in trouble.

"Please have him go to Mr. Ferguson's room when the bell rings."

Mr. Ferguson? My stomach drops. What is he going to say?

After class, I walk slowly because I don't want to run into Xander and everybody else.

Mr. Ferguson is out in the hallway, taping another mushroom cartoon to his door. The class is gone, except for Mosquito Boy, who is chattering away.

"Um, Trevor." Mosquito Boy stops and looks at me. "Why weren't you in class?"

Mr. Ferguson tells him that he'd like to talk with me in private and takes me inside. The earthy smell of the place makes me sad because I miss it already.

He gestures for me to sit down at the nearest lab table and he walks over to his desk, picks up a pink slip of paper, and sets it down in front of me.

DROP/ADD FORM
Student: Trevor Musgrove
Drop: Summit Science Investigations, FERGUSON, period 7.
Add: Science Investigations, BECKER, period 7.

"I received this in my box, and I haven't had a chance to talk to Ms. Beitz. What's this about?" he asks me.

He's going to make me say it out loud: *The reason I'm not in your class anymore is because I'm not smart enough.*

"Was this something you requested?" he asks.

"No. I'd like to stay."

"Then what's the problem?"

"I'm not in the Summit program."

"Ah. That is a problem." He pulls up a stool. "Did you apply?"

I shake my head. "I didn't know anything about it. Ms. Beitz said I was put in here because of a computer error."

The bell rings for the next class.

He reads my mind and tells me that he'll write me a pass so I won't be in trouble for being late.

We're both quiet for a second. The teacher across the hall yells at everybody to listen up and then her door slams shut.

He pulls down his glasses and looks at me over them. "There are rules, Mr. Musgrove. Admittance into Summit classes is by application only, and the application process is competitive."

"I know. Mr. Gonzalez told me."

He frowns. "I suggest you talk to Mr. Raye about this."

"Who is Mr. Raye?"

"Don't you have Mr. Raye for art? He teaches the regular art electives as well as Summit Art, and he's the Summit Program Coordinator."

"I don't have art. They gave me Computer Applications."

He makes a face. "Your schedule sounds like it needs major surgery, Mr. Musgrove. Based on the drawings of yours that I have seen, I suggest you advocate for Summit Art. Tell Mr. Raye that you'd like him to consider letting you into both Summit Art and Summit Science. It's never been done before, but that shouldn't keep you from trying."

"Sounded like rules are rules to me," I say.

He nods. "Sometimes rules are rules. And sometimes rules get overruled."

"You think I can get in?"

He shrugs. "Only one way to find out, Mr. Musgrove. Try. I will talk to Mr. Raye, but you should talk to him on your own. The purpose of the application process is to make sure that the students who get into the program are students who are motivated to be in it. If you want something badly enough, you owe it to yourself to try to get it."

"I'm motivated. I just didn't know about it."

He nods. "Tell that to Mr. Raye." He writes a

pass and hands it to me. I'm almost out the door when he says, "Wait . . ." He opens up a mini fridge and gives me a small paper bag. "This mushroom is at the right stage to release its spores. Make a spore print and see if you can identify it."

"You give out homework to kids even when they're not in your class anymore?"

He raises his eyebrows and his eyes twinkle. "I think you'll find it interesting."

A question that's been on my mind pops out. "I've been thinking about pod rot. . . . What stops a parasitic fungus from destroying everything that's alive? Once it gets going, why doesn't it destroy all the trees?"

"Ah." He smiles. "That's an interesting question. If a parasite kills its host—its primary means of survival—it no longer has food, so it essentially endangers itself. The ideal parasite doesn't kill its host. It evolves."

"What do you mean, it evolves?"

"It adapts in ways that won't undermine its own survival." He walks me to the door. "Discussion to be continued. You're going to be later than late.

Chapter three in the book! Read it. And, by the way, hope for some rain. A good soak will bring out more fungi." He waves me off.

"I'm perambulating!" I say, and hear his leprechaunic laugh behind me.

Maybe I should beg Mr. Raye for major surgery on my schedule.

I get to P.E. and everybody is running laps, and the sight of Xander rips the positive mood right out of me. I stay away from him and run my laps and when I see a chance with Langley, I ask him to tell The Plague's coach that I can't be on the team.

"Why?" Langley asks.

I can't tell him, so I just run on.

23.
JUAN

Nothing like babysitting after spending a humiliating day at school.

Mom is at the Fry Factory, frying fries. Michael and Tish are frying each other. Michael wants to draw another picture for Mom because he still wants her to buy him a stupid backpack, and Tish wants the crayon he's using.

"Stop arguing. Just forget about the picture. We're broke. It didn't work last time. It's not going to work this time."

I'm looking in my backpack for a pen when I run across the paper bag that Mr. Ferguson gave me. There's a mushroom in it with the instructions for making a spore print.

I cut off the stem, turn it over, and set it down on the paper. I don't know if it's going to work.

Tish tries to grab it.

"What is that?" Michael asks.

"It's homework for a class I don't even have."

"That's stupid."

"Yeah. Well, don't touch it."

I put the paper and the mushroom on top of the refrigerator next to Mom's orange shoe box and put a jelly jar over it.

That's the total of my Friday night excitement.

● ● ●

On Saturday I have to go to the library and wait in the line to get a computer in order to do my homework for Computer Applications. It takes forever. I hate that class.

When I come back home, everybody is in a bad mood. Even Tish, who would rather walk around with a load in her pants the size of Montana than try to use the potty.

Mom wants us all to sit on the potty and smile so Tish gets the idea that it's fun. I swear, this is what I'm being asked to do on Saturday night. I refuse, and Mom gets even more mad at me. It's like we're at war, only we're not saying it out loud.

On Sunday Michael demands that I check my "snore print," which I've forgotten about. I stand on a chair and look on top of the fridge. The mushroom is just sitting there. The paper around it is clean. Doesn't look like anything happened.

I take off the glass and lift the mushroom off.

Chocolate-brown spores have fallen straight down to make a pattern on the paper that matches the way the spores were on the gills of the mushroom. You can't see individual spores because they're too small. It's like the way a computer image is really made up of pixels.

I lift the print down carefully and set it on the table.

Michael forgets his bad mood for a brief moment to be in awe.

"It's called a spore print."

I'm going to press it in my Identification Notebook and show it to Mr. Ferguson on Monday. I don't know why. But I really like the fact that it worked.

● ● ●

After dinner there's a knock on the door. It's Juan. He's real shy and won't come in all the way.

Mom is sitting at the table circling job possibilities in the newspaper, and Michael and Tish are "helping" by drawing scribbles all over it.

"I think you should try out for the Toilers," Juan says, and he holds out a pair of cleats. "They're my cousin's. Too big for me. Too small for him." He shrugs. "I'm trying out."

"Is this the school team?" Mom asks.

Juan nods.

"Trevor, if you can be back by four forty-five so I can get to the Fry Factory, then that's fine," she says. "In fact, I think it's great. See, Trevor?" She shoots me a look. "I don't say no to everything you want."

She thinks being on the Toilets is just as good

as being on The Plague. She has no clue. I want to tell her what Langley and Xander said about the Toilets, but I don't because I don't want to burst Juan's bubble.

He backs into the hallway with a shrug. "I figure if you play on it, maybe we'd win. See you tomorrow."

"Thanks."

I close the door and try on a cleat. Not bad.

Maybe I should try out. But Xander said only the dregs are on the school team.

"Mom," I say. "What exactly does 'dreg' mean?"

She rips a page out of the newspaper. "Bottom of the barrel. The junk nobody wants. Why?"

"Just something I heard."

24.
BEGGING

Before first period, I hustle to the art hallway and work up the courage to enter Mr. Raye's room.

The door is open, there's reggae music playing, and a big huge dude with a head full of thick, twisted locks is tearing a giant piece of paper off a gigantic roll. It's like Jamaica's Paul Bunyan went to art school and became a teacher.

"What's up?" he asks.

I step in, but I'm momentarily occupied with my nostrils. There's that great smell, like the air is painted with primary colors. But I'm not here to fill up my smell bank, I'm here to beg.

"I'm Trevor Musgrove." Mr. Trevor Motivated Musgrove.

He sets the giant paper on a giant table and begins pulling another sheet off the giant roll. I go on, "I'm hoping you could do some major surgery on my schedule."

Okay, I stole the line, but it works. He looks up with a smile.

"I want to take Summit Art instead of Computer Applications and Mr. Ferguson's Summit Science Class instead of regular science. I just want you to know: I'm motivated. I am more motivated than anybody has ever been motivated in the history of motivation. Even my molecules have motivity."

He laughs. "Mr. Ferguson mentioned that you might be coming in."

He asks me a bunch of questions about where I went to school before and I try to be motivated and charming, and then he tells me that it isn't easy to get around the Summit application guidelines and that he'll have to get back to me.

The waiting game.

25.
NEWS

For a whole week it's like I'm walking on the edge of a cliff, wondering if I'll get the chance to switch my classes, wondering if I should try out for the Toilets, trying to avoid Xander and Diamond. On the weekend, it's more time at the library waiting in line to use the computer.

On Monday, while we're waiting for the bus, Juan is reminding me that Toilets tryouts are tomorrow when Diamond comes marching out dressed like a wannabe diva in makeup and a top with sequins on it. *"If you love me, baby, set me free,"* she sings. "Stars Show tryouts are today, so everybody here has to wish us luck."

"Luck? You need a miracle," Markus says.

Celine comes out next, looking like she's headed for death row.

Diamond yells, "Where's your top, Celine? You're supposed to wear your purple top."

"I'm not doing it," Celine says.

"Uh-oh." Markus holds up his hands. "Everybody back up, because the Krakatoa volcanoa is about to blowa."

Diamond's eyes go hard. "You can't just *not* do it, Celine. Tryouts are today."

Celine lays it down. "I'm not doing it, Diamond. I told you I'd chicken out."

"What am I supposed to do?"

"Do it without me."

"It's a *duet*, Celine. I can't sing your part and my part at the same time. And what about the moves? What am I supposed to do when I'm doing that lunge and you're doing your part?"

"Just do that lunge."

"That's boring! It won't look right. Come on, you promised." Diamond looks at me. "Don't you think she has to do it?"

I don't say a word. Ever since she messed up Xander's locker she's been trying to get back on my good side, but I'm like those dead presidents on Mount Rushmore. My face is a rock.

Markus steps in. "Celine has done abandoned you, Diamond. Get over it."

Diamond and Celine fight all the way to school. After my second class, I get called to see Ms. Beitz again.

Finally some news.

"Well, Trevor. Mr. Raye and Mr. Ferguson and I enjoyed a long discussion this morning." She drums her fingernails on her desk. Today, each nail has a fire-engine red background with black-yellow-and-orange sunburst designs painted on top. "Mr. Raye is willing to consider a special, late application to the Summit Program. He said you have to turn in something called . . ." She plucks a yellow sticky note from her desk and hands it to me.

*Kingdom of Fungi
Identification Notebook*

"Do you know what this is?" she asks.

I nod.

"The decision will be based on the drawings and notes in your notebook, as well as your grades from last year and a short essay that you need to write. Everything is explained here on this sheet. I've pulled last year's report card from your file and attached a copy of that. Fill out this form completely, attach the essay, and turn it in with your notebook to Mr. Raye or Mr. Ferguson by Monday. They will review it and make their decision based on the quality of your work."

"Thank you. Thank you. Thank you."

She holds out the form but grips it when I try to take it. "He didn't say yes, Trevor. He said they would *consider* it based on the quality of your work."

"I know. Thank you."

"Mr. Raye is bending the rules like this based on what Mr. Ferguson said about your potential, so I think you owe Mr. Ferguson a thank-you regardless of the outcome."

"I'll give him a huge thank-you."

She releases the form.

"And by the way, Ms. Beitz," I say in all sincerity, "I think each of your fingernails is like a little work of art."

Get ready for this . . . Ms. Beitz actually smiles.

I got it. I got it. Oh, yeah. Oh, yeah. I got it.

Mr. Trevor Finesse Musgrove is back!

I got it. I got it. Oh, yeah. Oh, yeah. I got it.

She writes me a pass.

I got it. I got it. Oh, yeah. Oh, yeah. I got it.

As I'm walking to my next class, I glance at last year's grades. Not great. But my notebook can make up for that. I'll do another entry or two. Put in some quality drawings and observations. I'm right near Mr. Ferguson's room, so I stop in.

He's standing on a chair, lifting a bagful of mushrooms off a ceiling hook.

"I just heard that I can apply."

Over his glasses he gives me one of his looks. "I'm sticking my neck out for you, Mr. Musgrove," he says. "I expect you to come through."

"I will. Thank you, Mr. Fungus."

It just pops out.

"Uh—I meant Mr. Ferguson."

He raises his eyebrows as he gets down.

"It's a compliment, Mr. Ferguson. I mean that."

He smiles. "You may perambulate to the egress, Mr. Mushroom."

During lunch, I sit with Juan and make another entry in my notebook. Langley stops by and says hey to both of us and cracks a joke. It's what you call a nice gesture, because basically Langley is a nice guy. Ever since the thing with Xander's locker, I haven't even tried sitting at the Summit table. Langley doesn't say anything about that, but his stopping by says a lot.

Diamond stops by, too, and tells me she wants me to draw a logo on her arm so she has good luck at auditions after school. She waves a five-dollar bill in my face. "Come on, Trevor. I'm gonna need it without Celine."

I tell her I'm busy.

MORCHELLA ANGUSTICEPS

Common name: BLACK MOREL

After a forest fire, everything is pretty much burned and dead. But guess what pops up first? Mushrooms. Morels most often because mycelia can survive a fire underground. When the mushrooms pop up, they smell good (or at least that's what bugs think) and so bugs come to eat the mushrooms, and the animals come to eat the bugs, and mushrooms and animals fertilize the ground and stuff starts to grow again.

YUMMY!

26.
THE BIG DAY BEGINS

All last night I went back and forth in my mind about whether to try out or not. This morning, the sky is cluttered up with clouds like it has a lot on its mind, too. Mr. Ferguson is probably hoping it rains, but I bet everybody who is trying out for soccer is hoping it doesn't.

By the time I get to the bus stop, Juan is already there, sitting on the fence, his leg jiggling like there's a motor in it.

"You decide about tryouts?" he asks.

I show him the cleats in my backpack.

He's not a slap-on-the-back, jump-up-and-down,

shout-out kind of guy. But in his quiet way, he looks like I just gave him a Christmas present.

Markus shuffles up and asks what's happening, and Juan tells him we're both trying out for soccer.

"Go Go, Toilets," Markus says. "Flush them babies down."

"Good luck," Diamond says, which makes me feel kind of bad because she sounds like she means it, and I didn't say anything to her yesterday. Then she adds, "You'll make it. I probably didn't even make the Stars Show."

"Stop saying that," Celine yells. "You're just trying to make me feel bad."

"Catfight!" Markus yells, and they both go after him.

As soon as we get to school, Juan begs me to come to the cafeteria so he can tell Javier that I'm trying out for the Toilets.

Javier shakes my hand. "Good decision, man. I'm the iron curtain. And we got the striker here and the roadrunner." He points to Juan. "Hey, we should get Langley. No way I want Xander. He's a ball hog, but Langley would be sweet."

"I figured it out," Juan says. "The coach said twenty is the max he wants on the team. There are ten eighth graders from last year who have to make it and six really good new eighth graders. So that leaves four spaces for seventh graders. If Langley and Xander try out, I won't make it."

"Xander's too good for the Toilets," Javier says. "Besides, you're fast, Juan. You run faster than the roadrunner, man. Beep-beep."

After breakfast, we catch Langley by his locker.

"Musgrove is trying out for the team," Javier says.

Langley looks at me.

I smile. "Toilets, here I come."

"Me and Trevor and Juan are all trying out. Come on, McCloud," Javier says.

We look at each other. Langley. Javier. Juan. And me.

I make the sound of a flush and swish my butt around like it's the water going around the bowl. Everybody cracks up. "It's our victory dance."

"The way I look at it, the more soccer the better." Langley does the victory dance, and we shake.

27.
NERVES

Everybody is nervous and jumpy. The people who tried out yesterday for the talent show are all gossiping about when the list of acts that made it will get posted. And all the people trying out for the soccer team keep talking about who's going to show up and who isn't. It's like the air today is invisibly threaded with electricity and we're all plugged in.

Diamond passes me a note in math class: *RU still mad about Xander's locker? What can I do to make it up to u?*

I throw it away.

At the end of the day, she sees me on the way to P.E. "Hey, Trevor, wait!" she calls out. "I got you something."

I pretend I don't hear and run ahead.

Langley is talking to Javier and Juan in the doorway to the gym. Juan looks like he's going to throw up.

"What's wrong?"

"I'm never going to make it now," Juan says. "Xander's trying out."

Langley shrugs. "I told him I was going to try out, and the next thing I know he's calling home to say he's going to stay after and try out, too."

"I knew it," Juan says.

Xander appears so we shut up and head in like it's just a regular day.

"I bet he won't come," I whisper to Juan.

28.
UNEXPECTED BLOW

After school, everybody who is trying out for soccer has to meet on the field. I dump my backpack in the pile of backpacks by the bleachers and jog over to where Coach Stevins is marking down names on a clipboard. It would be nice if he smiled, like he's happy I showed up, but he's into his refrigerator state, not giving up anything for anybody.

Juan and Javier are there. Langley and Xander aren't.

The sky is gray and dark clouds are gathering right above the field.

The coach looks at his watch. "Okay, people, let's get going in case it rains. Everybody is—"

Langley comes jogging out with Xander.

Juan shakes his head.

"Sorry we're late," Langley says to Stevins.

Stevins nods, which is a real little motion since he's got no neck, and he keeps his refrigerator face on, but I think I see a little smile. "I was just saying that everybody here is in the same boat. I'm going to judge you on skills and speed and teamwork. Soccer is a team sport."

Soccer is a team sport, but every coach probably wants a star like Xander on his team. They want to get the goals any way they can.

He takes us through some warm-ups and then sets up a drill. "Do we have any keepers?" he asks.

Javier raises his hand along with two others.

"You can go first." He throws a pair of goalie gloves at Javier. "We'll do a simple shooting drill. One line. First in line passes to me and runs around to the side. When I pass it back, take a shot on Javier here."

We go.

Javier is calm and confident, on his toes, making save after save.

Xander's turn. He rips it.

Javier dives but the shot is too hard and fast to block.

Xander smiles.

The coach tries a few other keepers, but nobody is as solid as Javier.

Scrimmage time. There are so many guys trying out, we have to split into four teams.

I end up on Xander's team.

He won't pass it to me, even when I'm wide open. He loses the ball three times.

"Pass the ball," an eighth grader says.

"If I see a shot, I'd be stupid not to take it," Xander argues.

I look over to see how Juan and Langley are doing.

"Hey!" Diamond's voice rings out. "Go, Toilets!" She's cheering from the bleachers and when I look, she points down to the pile of backpacks like she's trying to tell me something.

"It's your girlfriend," Xander says to me under his breath.

Rise above it.

"Xander," I say. "We're on the same team here. Maybe if you'd pass, we could score."

"Hey, I'm trying to score. I don't see you taking any decent shots." He gets the ball and plows ahead.

"Xander!" a guy on our team calls. Left wing. Our defender in the back is open, too, and in a great position to chip it over to me. I imagine that I'm up high looking down on the field and I see all these possible connections, like there are invisible streets going from one player to another that the ball could travel on, a hundred different possible paths to the goal. But every time Xander gets possession he dribbles it down a dead-end alley and runs into a wall.

This is exactly what The Plague's coach meant when he said you have to watch the whole field and not just the ball.

Coach Stevins walks from field to field. How can he even see what I've got? All this energy is rumbling inside me and if I could just connect with the ball, I know I could send it flying down the right path to get a goal.

He mixes things up and we play one more scrimmage, then it's time to go.

He dismisses everybody except Langley, Xander, me, and three eighth graders.

"I haven't picked any players yet," he says. "I just need some information from you guys because I know you're all on travel teams. I need to know whether your practices for your teams will conflict with the Toilers. I have a limited number of slots and I don't want to give one to somebody who isn't going to be able to show. Our games will either be on Tuesdays or Thursdays. Our practices will be on Mondays and Tuesdays and Thursdays when we don't have games."

Langley is the first to speak up. "All The Plague games are on Saturdays and we practice on Wednesdays and Fridays."

"Soccer almost every day?" The Refrigerator smiles. "Can you take it?"

Langley smiles back.

The other players give him information about their teams. Then it's my turn to let him know that I won't be playing on The Plague.

The coach writes it all down and dismisses us.

I don't want to miss the activity bus so I hustle. I pick up my backpack and start to take off.

Xander suddenly starts going crazy. "Where's my cell phone?"

Coach Stevins puts down his clipboard. "You had it here?"

"In my backpack. Somebody had to have taken it. It couldn't just disappear."

Stevins's voice snaps into action. "Okay, people, Xander's cell phone is missing. Everybody take a look around you."

A bad feeling creeps into me. I have nothing to do with Xander's cell phone, but I have this feeling that Xander thinks I did it.

"Hey," Xander says. "I had to call home right after school. I think I might have forgotten to turn it off. Langley, call my number. Maybe it'll ring."

Langley dials his phone.

There's a long pause while the number goes out

there looking for the phone. I'm flashing back to what Diamond said earlier about how she got me something, and I'm remembering her pointing to the backpacks.

And then it happens. The sound of Xander's ringtone.

Everybody looks at me because it's coming from my backpack.

29.
GUILTY UNTIL PROVEN INNOCENT

Coach Stevins takes me and Xander to Mr. Gonzalez's office. Mr. Gonzalez wants to talk about it, but the activity bus is coming and that's my only ride home.

I say I'm not guilty, and he says I'll get to tell him my side of the story first thing in the morning. In the meantime, he says, he's calling my mom and we should talk about it tonight.

Nobody on the bus knows anything, because they were already gone by the time it happened. I keep my mouth shut and sit down. Lucky this isn't our regular bus because I could not handle Diamond right now. I know she did it, and if I had to deal with her on this bus, I'd get a lifetime of detentions.

"You made it, didn't you?" Juan says. He thinks the reason I'm late is because I got good news. "You, Langley, Xander, and those eighth graders for sure."

I won't talk about it. He wants to know what's wrong, but he leaves me alone.

As soon as the bus pulls up, I run over to Diamond's building. I'm going to drag her to my apartment by the hair if I have to, and she's going tell my mom what she did. If Diamond wouldn't have interfered, everything would be fine. I need favors from Diamond Follet like I need a bullet hole in my brain.

I knock on the door. No answer. I knock again and yell Diamond's name.

"She ain't here!" Mudman's voice shouts back, and then he swears at me.

I look around Deadly Gardens for a while, but nobody has seen her.

Nothing to do but go home.

When I open the door to our apartment, Mom is standing at the stove. She's got Tish on one hip, and she's stirring something. Rex is sitting on the floor banging a pot with a spoon.

"I didn't do it."

She keeps looking at the soup. "I can't tell you how—" Her voice cracks, and she clears her throat. Rex starts banging the cupboard door, and she takes the spoon away from him. "Soon as Lily picks up Rex, I have to go to the Fry Factory. We will talk about this when I get home."

Rex starts crying.

From the bathroom, Michael calls out, "I can't find it, Mom!"

"Just a minute, Michael!" she yells back.

"Mom, let me just explain what—"

"Hundreds of dollars. That's how much Mr. Gonzalez said the phone is worth. Hundreds of dollars. That's not a little thing. It's a big crime, Trevor. You have no idea how—"

"I didn't do it!"

She puts down Tish, picks up Rex, and heads

for the bathroom. "You know what, Trevor? I said I can't handle this now, and I mean it. We'll talk about it when I get back."

Lily comes and Mom does her fake smile and hands over Rex. As soon as they leave, she stomps around the apartment, giving orders, and then she's out the door.

Somehow I get through Michael's and Tish's whining. I put a note on the kitchen table.

I know it looks bad, but I didn't take the phone. You have to believe me. Here's what I think happened. I think Diamond Follet took Xander's phone and put it in my backpack. The day after The Plague try-outs, she overheard Xander insult me, and she wrote a curse word on his locker. She thought she was doing me a favor, but I got in trouble for it and got mad at her. She's been trying to get back on my good side ever since. Yesterday she told me that she had something for me, and then she showed up at the soccer tryouts, where all the backpacks were, and she pointed at my backpack. I swear I didn't ask her to take the phone. I didn't ask her to do anything but leave me alone. Please believe me.

When my mom comes home, I pretend I'm asleep. The lock turns, backpack plops, footsteps move into the kitchen, chair legs scrape against the floor. It's quiet. She's reading my letter.

My stomach ties itself in a knot.

After a while she whispers, "Trev, you awake?"

She wants to talk about it.

Yeah, I should say, *I'm awake.* But I can't. All the pressures of the day are squeezing the breath out of me.

30.
THE DREGS

In the morning, my mom wakes me up. "We have to talk," she says, and sits me down at the table.

I'm not even awake yet.

"I don't know what to believe," she says. Her face is saggy, like she got older overnight. "Have you talked to Diamond about this? Has she admitted anything?"

I shake my head.

My mom goes on. "Let's say it's true about her. If so, then—"

"It is true, Mom."

She sighs. "What are you going to tell Mr. Gonzalez?"

"I'm going to say I didn't do it."

* ● ●

At the bus stop, I don't say anything to anybody.

When I get to the office, Xander is already there with his dad, waiting in the chairs by Mr. Gonzalez's door. His dad is tall with brown hair, just like Xander's. He's got designer-looking clothes—black jeans and a cool blue shirt. I remember Xander saying he's a photographer. Maybe he's a famous one.

Xander whispers something, and his dad looks at me.

Mr. Gonzalez steps out of his office and Xander's dad breaks into a smile. They shake hands.

"A pleasure to meet you, Mr. Gonzalez," Xander's dad says. "I'm Alexander Pierce."

"Yes, yes," Gonzalez says. "Thank you so much for all your work on the Web site. The photos are amazing. Everyone's talking about it."

Mr. Pierce waves one hand. "It was nothing. Happy to do it."

Mr. Gonzalez takes them into his office. His voice is too soft to hear, but Mr. Pierce's laugh rings out. "Sure, we can get this straightened out quickly. . . . Not the one to throw stones," Mr. Pierce is saying. "The boy . . . Well . . . not exactly trustworthy." Another laugh. "Yes . . . I heard he had a phone and lost it. . . . This used to be a solid neighborhood. . . . It was a mistake to redraw the boundary lines. . . . We've been supporting . . . more than our share . . . seriously consider sending Alexander to private school . . . shouldn't have to worry about having things stolen. . . ."

Mr. Gonzalez talks awhile, and then Mr. Pierce's voice comes through again: "Let's be honest, the people from those apartments are the dregs. . . . Xander should be surrounded by a peer group that lifts him up, not one that drags him down."

After another long minute, the door opens and they walk out. I pretend like I'm getting something out of my backpack so I don't have to look at them. My face is burning.

Mr. Gonzalez brings me into his office. "Your

mom called right before the Pierces arrived. She's coming in tomorrow morning so that we can all sit down and talk about this together. She told me about the note you wrote. So you believe that Diamond stole the phone and put it in your backpack?"

"I didn't do it. Somebody had to."

He looks tired, like I just handed him another problem that he doesn't want to deal with. "Mr. Pierce was asking if we should involve the police."

The bottom falls out of my stomach.

"Since the phone is undamaged and back in Xander's possession, I'd like to keep this a school matter, but I want you to understand that stealing is a crime."

"I do."

"If I call Diamond in here, what do you think she's going to say?"

"I don't know."

He sighs and looks out the window like he wishes he could jump out and keep running. I wouldn't want his job, either.

After a few seconds he turns back. "First thing

in the morning, we're all going to sit down together. Diamond, too."

He tells me that I have to go to class.

I keep my mouth shut and go to my locker. I'm shaking. I'm unloading the stuff from my back-pack when I notice it: my Fungi Identification Notebook is missing. I was planning on working on it at lunch.

I check my locker and backpack three times.

Great. This day just gets better and better.

31.
DIAMOND

By the time I get to Computer Applications, word about Xander's cell phone showing up in my backpack is out. I can tell. It's like somebody painted a giant bull's-eye on my back, because everybody is aiming glances at me.

U.S. History next. Diamond is in that class. When I walk in, she hustles over and says, "I heard about the phone. What did you say to Gonzalez?"

Javier turns to listen.

I refuse to answer.

During math she gets called to the office. I'm

sitting there, staring at these equations that I'm supposed to be solving, but I'm imagining her in with Mr. Gonzalez. She's going to kill me. She's going to tell everybody that I'm just trying to pin it on her. I can't win.

She comes back faster than I expected and looks scared. When the teacher isn't looking, she slips me a note:

Mr. G asked questions about Xander's phone. I told him I didn't know anything about it. What's going on? RU trying to get back at me for the locker?

I tear the note to pieces and brush them off my desk.

When lunchtime rolls around, I pretend like I'm not a walking target for gossip. I sit down with my tray, my back to the Summit table. Juan slides in opposite me.

"Rumors are flying," he says.

"Yeah," I say.

"Did you do it?" he asks.

"Nope."

I don't say any more, and he doesn't, either.

I am glad he's there, though. Because it would look really pathetic if I was sitting all by myself.

Diamond is huddled at the far end of the Deadly Gardens table with Celine. On the way out, Celine comes over and says, "Diamond needs to know what's going on."

I look her right in the eye. "Diamond needs to figure out things for herself."

I get through English and science. We have an assembly last period, which saves me from having to go to P.E. with Xander and Diamond. Next thing I know, I'm getting on the bus.

Markus is right behind me. "Heard you got caught, man. You need some lessons from the master. Doesn't do you any good to steal a cell phone. They can always just kill it or trace your calls."

I tell Markus to give his little lesson to Diamond, and I sit in the back.

Diamond and Celine get on.

Markus yells, "Diamond, what's up with Xander's phone?"

Diamond throws her backpack on the seat.

"I don't know why everybody's looking at me. I didn't do nothing."

The bus takes off, and all this rage just rumbles around and around in my brain. By the time the bus pulls up to Deadly Gardens, I can't stand it anymore. I follow Diamond to her building.

"Oooh," Markus says. "There they go."

I shout back at him to shut up. Then I yell, "Why'd you do it, Diamond?"

"I don't know what you're talking about." Diamond walks in the front door of her building.

I head in after her. "I'm not going down for what you did, Diamond."

In the middle of the ground-floor hallway, she drops her backpack and turns around to face me, putting her hands on her hips. "What did I do?"

"You stole, Diamond. It's a crime."

She gets all huffy. "I didn't steal it, for your information. It was a present. I was just trying to be nice. Go ahead and kill me—"

"Stop lying. You stole it from Xander, and we both know it."

"It wasn't Xander's. I got it from Mr. Raye."

"Right. Mr. Raye gave you a cell phone."

"No! The marker. He gave me the marker I put in your backpack. . . ." She yanks my backpack around and unzips the small front pouch and pulls out a silver marker. "It's for your designs. Silver. Mr. Raye said I could have it because I helped him clean up. I don't know nothing about Xander's cell phone." She sticks the pen in her backpack.

She got a marker from Mr. Raye and put it in my backpack at tryouts. That was the "something" she said she was getting me. A gift. She didn't steal Xander's phone.

32.
HELP

I don't know what to do or what to say. I was so sure she had done it. In a daze, I turn around and walk back toward the front door.

"Thanks a lot, Trevor!" she yells.

A door bangs open.

Mudman's voice slices through the air like a rusty blade. "I thought I heard you. You little piece of—"

Next thing I know, she's running for the front door. He bulldozes past me like I'm not even there. Before she makes it out, he grabs her and pulls her down the stairs toward the laundry room.

"You're in trouble again, you—" he yells, and she's trying to say something, and this strange feeling is taking over me from the inside out. Then there's this bad noise like a crack that makes me jump. I'm running down the stairs even though it doesn't feel like my legs are working. I have no plan, no idea what I'm doing. But my legs are fueled with that stuff that runs through your veins and makes you strong in emergencies. Adrenaline. It's like the adrenaline is activating another *me* that's inside of the scared me, a *me* that is running toward Mudman instead of away from him. I run into the basement hallway and he's holding Diamond's arm with one hand and his other hand is in the air, and I still don't know what I'm doing, but my voice rings out. "Stop!"

My voice surprises him. It's that simple. He didn't expect it, and he lets go of her to look at me. Diamond takes off for the back door. I take off for the front. I'm running again. My mind is running fast, too. I'm hoping that for a second he didn't know which way to run and that one second might give us what we need to get away. I run around the building and see Diamond running toward me. Mudman is behind her, yelling. We can't go to my apartment or he'll know where I live. I head toward the parking lot, and Diamond catches up. We're running together now. Only one guy is out, waiting at the bus stop, and he doesn't speak English. Mudman is coming. I pull Diamond across the street, and just as he steps off the curb to cross, a car comes. He steps back and curses.

"This way!" I pull Diamond down a path that heads over to Clover Park, another apartment complex across from Deadly Gardens.

We run in between the buildings without looking back and cross two more roads until we get to the stoplight on Branch Road. Neither of us have any breath left, and we're both shaking.

The *me* that was full of adrenaline is fading fast. I keep looking to see if Mudman is following.

Diamond can't talk. She's bending over, holding on to her other arm.

"You okay?" I ask.

She stays like that for a long time. Her arm— the one I wasn't holding—doesn't look right at all, like it's out of place in a funny way. When she finally straightens up, I see her face and I have to look away real fast.

I always thought of Diamond's face as hard, but it's not. It's soft, and the whole left side is bleeding.

The light is green and the WALK sign is flashing. I don't know what to do. My heart is pounding, and my lungs feel like a knife is stuck in them. Diamond is bent over again and she's crying in a real funny way like I once heard a sick puppy cry and she's holding her arm and isn't talking at all.

Cars are going by, and a woman sitting in the passenger's side of one car sees that Diamond is hurt, but the car keeps going.

We can't go back to Deadly Gardens.

I don't know what to do. There's an apartment building across the street. Should I go over there and get somebody to help us? Two blocks over is a playground. Maybe I should run over there and see if anybody is around.

Diamond is still bent over, holding her arm,

and she's got her shoulder all scrunched up so I can't see her face, but the sleeve of her white top is smeared with blood. I don't have anything in my pocket to give her. Not a single tissue or anything.

Another car drives by. Maybe I should flag it. I look back, expecting to see Mudman. Two more cars pass, but the people in them don't look nice.

Finally I see a police car. I hold up my arm like the guys in the movies do when they're flagging down a taxi, which strikes me as funny, only it's not.

"No!" she says, scared.

It's too late. The cop pulls over.

"Trevor, no!" Diamond says. She tries to straighten up and puts her good hand on her eye, but letting go of her arm must hurt because she moans and bends over again and holds it, her hand red with blood. I am glad she's bent over because I can't look at her face. She takes two steps back like she's going to run away, but then she moans again and blood is coming out from underneath her hand.

"She needs help!" I'm screaming at the cop.

He is walking toward us, pulling out his two-way radio, calling for an ambulance.

"No!" Diamond says, but she crumples onto the sidewalk.

"What happened?" The policeman looks at me, and I say that a guy just beat her up and we were running away from him. He asks if we know the guy and does he have a weapon and where did it happen, and Diamond doesn't want to say anything. She just cries. Right away the guy calls for backup and for a "female unit" to go to the hospital, and then he crouches down next to her.

"Where does it hurt most?" he asks.

She doesn't answer. She just cries.

He's so calm, like a nice robot cop. "An ambulance is coming. Can you tell me exactly what happened?"

I explain how I went looking for Diamond in Deadly Gardens and how Mudman came and the more I talk, the bigger the lump gets in my throat. . . . Finally I just say it.

"It's my fault."

The cop looks up. "Why is it your fault?"

"I got her in trouble at school and that's why the guy came after her."

Diamond shakes her head. "Derrick don't need an excuse, Trevor."

"Has Derrick done this before?" the cop asks.

Diamond shuts up.

"Has he hit you before?"

"He's gonna be mad if he gets in trouble . . . ," Diamond says, and then her voice disappears. She starts to get up like she's just going to walk away, but the cop gently makes her sit back down again and asks for a description of Derrick and her address.

She closes her lips together.

"Is there anybody else at home who might be in danger? A mother or a brother or sister?" the cop asks.

Diamond won't answer.

The cop doesn't say anything. He just shifts his weight, still crouched—his black shoes perfectly shined—and waits patiently for Diamond to answer.

Real softly in the distance, a siren moans.

Diamond gives him her address and tells him what Derrick looks like. The cop says she made the right decision and he's going to make sure that they protect the rest of her family, and he calls in the address.

How can he promise that? I don't know what Diamond is thinking, but I'm thinking about how fast Mudman hurt Diamond, and I'm wondering how fast the cops can possibly get there.

The ambulance turns down Branch Road and pulls up. How many times have I seen an ambulance and wondered what it was for. This time I know. The police officer steps aside, and two guys hop out and take over. They ask Diamond a few questions and help her on this stretcher thing, and the next thing I know I'm watching them close the doors. Another cop car pulls up with two cops in it and our cop talks to them, and then they take off toward Deadly Gardens. The cop asks for my phone number, but he doesn't get through so he asks for my address. "Mom or dad at home?" he asks.

"My mom," I say.

He says something to his radio I don't understand, and then says they'll need to get a statement from me at the station because I'm a witness and they'll send a car over to my mom, too.

I freak out because Mom is going to freak out and I try to explain about how my mom has to work and I have to babysit Tish and Michael, and the cop talks into the radio again and then he tells me that he can take me home and get the statement there. I get in the backseat, which smells like toilet bowl cleaner and is perfectly free of any litter. I mean there's not a gum wrapper, not a rubber band, not a cigarette butt, not a speck of dust. Every night this police officer must wipe away all the traces of the bad guys who get put in this backseat. Mud and blood and beer and grease. Who knows what's all been in this car. The dregs. And now there's me in it. I get all outraged at Xander for blaming something on me that I didn't do, and I turn around and do the same thing to Diamond.

I wish I could have at least told Diamond I was

sorry for jumping to conclusions about her stealing the phone.

I'm hot and hungry and thirsty. I wish this car
came with a mini fridge, but you can't be giving
cold drinks to criminals. That's why it's so clean.
You don't want to be giving a criminal anything,
not even a stubby old pencil, because you never
know how he might turn it against you. That's the
power of clean.

I wish somebody would come every night and
clean up Deadly Gardens so that it was clean like
this car. If I had a car this clean I wouldn't even
bother sleeping in Deadly Gardens. I'd just live
in this car. I'd take real good care of it. No trash.
I'd keep four things in it at all times. Number
one: a soccer ball, because you never know when
you're going to get a chance to play. Numbers two
and three: a blank book, real thick paper with no
lines, and a set of fine-point permanent markers,
because you never know when inspiration is going
to strike. And number four: a mini fridge stocked
with nice cold drinks.

At a stoplight the cop types in something on

this laptop that is attached to the dashboard and another call comes in on the radio and he talks cop lingo back. I wonder what kind of information is on that computer? I can't see the screen, so I don't know what he's looking at. I gave him my name and address. Does it say stuff in there about my mom? Does it say that my dad is in jail?

My dad must have been in the backseat of at least one police car. Probably more than one. Was he sick to his stomach, too? Was he sorry for what he did or just sorry he got caught?

On the back of the seat right behind the cop, I notice a slice in the vinyl. It's like somebody stuck a knife blade right in the backseat while Mr. Nice Robot Cop was driving. I hope it wasn't my dad who did it, but maybe it was.

I try to imagine that I'm a cop and I have to go to Diamond's place and kick open the door and there's Mudman waiting for me with a knife or a gun. I wonder if Mr. Nice Robot Cop feels lucky that he was assigned the easy job of taking me home and somebody else is stuck with the job of getting Mudman?

The cop looks at me in the rearview mirror. "You did the right thing flagging me down."

The lump in my throat is back.

"If this is a case of ongoing abuse, that girl's right. The guy didn't need an excuse. He'd find a reason. Believe me. Guys like that are just sick, so don't take it on."

I hear what he's saying, but I still feel rotten.

33.
MOM'S REACTION

When we pull in to the Deadly Gardens parking lot, I slide down real low just in case Mudman is out and he wants to kill me. He could be hiding in the bushes or behind the Dumpster, watching. The cop doesn't seem to be afraid. Maybe one of those radio calls told him that they got Mudman. The other cop car is already in the parking lot, so maybe those guys are up in Diamond's apartment making an arrest.

It's Michael who opens the door, and when he sees Officer Robocop, he runs straight into the back bedroom.

"Trevor?" Mom walks out of the bathroom with Tish on one hip and when she sees us, she almost faints. She's got on her Fry Factory uniform, looking like her worst nightmare just came true.

Nice Robocop gets right to the point. "Your son witnessed a domestic violence situation and flagged us for help."

"What? I thought he was in trouble at school." She starts talking about Mr. Gonzalez and I interrupt her. Last thing I need is for the cops to find out I'm the chief suspect in a cell phone theft. Quickly I tell Mom the Diamond story. Then Mom has a billion questions for him, and he answers all the ones he can. Another guy comes who says he's a detective and he asks me more questions and then he has questions for Mom, so I take Tish and sit at the kitchen table. Tish twists herself around so she can keep an eye on Mr. Nice Cop and all the gear attached to his belt—the cell phone, the radio, the big blunt gun—and on his perfectly unwrinkled uniform. How is it that cops run around all day fighting crime and they never have any wrinkles or stains on their clothes? Maybe they wash their stuff in a special stain-protective, wrinkle-protective soap.

The cop gets a call and he steps into the hallway to take it. My mom just gives me this look like she doesn't know what to think, but the detective is still asking questions. Then the cop comes back in and he looks glad and he tells us that they have made an arrest. Mom has a hundred more questions, and he gives her a phone number and explains how she can get more information, and the detective says that they might need to ask us more questions later.

"Is Diamond okay?" I ask.

"My guess is a broken arm," Mr. Nice Cop says. "She'll be okay. Listen, if you're ever a witness to anything like this again, do me a big favor and get adult help first, okay? You could have gotten hurt trying to intervene."

They leave, and Mom just stands there facing the door. She's turning herself into a statue so she won't cry.

"Mom—"

She doesn't move.

"Mom, I'm sorry."

She says to the door, "I don't even know what to be upset about. I'm glad you're okay. But I'm just overwhelmed by everything, Trevor."

Tish climbs down from my lap and goes over and hugs her leg. "What time is it?" Mom looks at the clock on the stove. "I'm late."

"I know. I'm sorry—"

She picks Tish up. "How can I go now?"

"It's okay. I'll watch Michael and Tish."

She shakes her head. "I'll be too worried—where's Michael? Michael?" She runs into the bathroom. "Michael? Trevor, where'd he go?"

I go into the bedroom. He's hiding behind the door.

Mom hands me Tish and picks him up. "Oh my Lord, you weigh a ton, baby."

He breaks into tears.

"Shh, it's okay. The cop wasn't mad at Trevor. He was mad at the bad guy and they got him."

"I thought he was coming for me."

"For you?" She carries him over and sits down in the kitchen. "Trevor, get him some toilet paper so he can blow his nose." She takes out her cell phone.

Michael sniffs. "Who you calling?"

She calls the Fry Factory and tells them she can't come in and I can tell by her conversation that whoever she's talking to doesn't like it, and after she hangs up her lips close real tight.

"What's wrong?" Michael asks.

She keeps her lips tight and just shakes her head.

Michael and Tish are both scared. It's easier when she yells and screams. When she's real quiet, it gets us all upset because it's like somebody has replaced our real mom with this statue mom.

Her voice finally comes out in a thin line: "You know me, Trevor. I don't like to talk about things when I'm upset. I have to think some things through. Either we'll talk about it when certain people are asleep, or first thing in the morning."

She cooks macaroni and cheese and nobody eats, and she doesn't talk at all, and then she just gets up and takes all the clothes and starts washing them in the bathtub like if she can just get them clean everything will turn out all right.

34.
THE REAL CRIMINAL

I'm thinking about Diamond and Mudman, and I'm thinking about the cell phone, too. If Diamond didn't put it in my backpack, who did? I can only think of one person.

There's a knock on the door and I freeze.

From the bathroom, Mom says, "What was that?"

The knock comes again, and Mom runs in with wet socks in her hands. "Don't open it," she whispers.

Juan calls my name from behind the door.

"It's Juan," I say.

He asks if he can talk to me, and Mom says he has to come in and then locks the door.

"Markus saw you in a cop car," he whispers after Mom goes back to her washing. "What happened, man?"

I retell the whole story.

He takes it all in. "Is Diamond okay?"

"I think so."

"If she didn't put the phone in your backpack, who did?"

I'm not sure how to answer. Accusing Diamond without proof was my last big mistake.

"You think somebody did it on purpose?"

"I think whoever did it wanted to make me look bad in front of Coach Stevins."

My mom is listening, even though she's pretending to put wet socks on the windowsill.

Juan's eyes light up. "Xander. He has it in for you, man."

"I don't have proof, but he's got the motive and he had the chance. Remember between scrimmages, he went over and got his water bottle?"

Juan shakes his head. "Man, that's going way too far. If he did and everybody finds out he stooped that low, he's gonna look bad for life. What are you going to do?"

"I already told Gonzalez I didn't do it. If I accuse Xander and he didn't do it, he'll make my life even more miserable."

"Yeah." Juan shakes his head again. "I bet Gonzalez wouldn't believe you even if it is true. Nobody would suspect Xander. He's like Straight A, Perfect Boy." He gives me a sympathetic shrug.

"Hey, Juan, don't tell anybody about Xander. Let me figure this out first."

He nods.

After he's gone, Mom walks in.

"Who is this Xander?"

"I've been trying to tell you. He's this guy who has it in for me."

"Why does he have it in for you?"

"I don't know. 'Cause I beat him at juggling. 'Cause I'm friends with Langley. 'Cause he just hates me. I don't know."

"Momma, Tish needs you!" Michael yells from the bathroom.

"You didn't steal the cell phone?"

"I didn't steal the cell phone."

She looks at me.

"I'm telling the truth."

She nods.

"Momma . . ."

"I'm coming, Michael! Trevor, you have to explain all this at that meeting tomorrow morning."

"I'm going to say I didn't do it, and they probably won't believe me."

She sighs. "I'm no good at meetings, Trev. You know that. It's like I'm afraid that every word that comes out of my mouth sounds stupid . . . I'll be there, but I don't know how much good I'm gonna do. I'm not one of those parents who can walk in and snap her fingers and make everything go the way she wants." Her voice catches on itself.

Tish starts to cry.

"Momma, Tish peed her pants."

"Great," Mom says. "More clothes to wash."

35.
THE NOTEBOOK

I am alone in the living room, lying on my mattress in the dark, looking out the window. When you're lying on your back, you can't see the ground or any trash. You just see the sky. Tonight, the gray fingers of a cloud are trying to suffocate the yellow moon. Every once in a while a streak of lightning shocks the darkness without any thunder, without any sign yet of rain.

A thousand thoughts are tangled up together in my mind. I'm thinking about Diamond and wondering if she's still in the hospital. I'm trying to imagine what it was like for her, living with Mudman. I remember that time she knocked on our door and asked to come in. I wish I had said yes.

The cop said guys like Mudman will find any excuse to beat up somebody. What kind of person wants to do that? How can that make him feel better?

That's why I don't understand Xander. He makes people feel bad all the time. It's not just me. He puts other people down, too. I don't understand how that could possibly make him feel good.

I'm going to have to face Xander and his dad at the meeting. Xander's dad is going to give me a look like "Here's one of the dregs." He's going to look at me and see a stupid, low-quality kid who is dragging his son's school down.

My mom always says judge people based on what they do, not what they have. Mr. Ferguson is like that. To Mr. Ferguson everybody is a fresh specimen, just waiting to be identified. You either earn his respect or you don't.

The thought of not being in his class anymore makes me sad. If somebody told me that my favorite class of all time would be taught by a mushroom-loving leprechaun, I would've thought, *No way*. But all you have to do is walk into his room and you know that something interesting is going on. Now there's not one thing that I have to look forward to. The only other decent class— P.E.—has Xander in it, so that's going to be about as much fun as running barefoot laps on broken glass.

Another bolt zigzags from one cloud to another, lighting up the sky.

I hold myself silent to hear if it's raining and wonder if Mr. Ferguson is looking out his window, hoping for "a good soak." I don't know how long I'm listening, but after a while I hear something. Not rain. Someone is crying, real faint.

I get up and look out the window. The street-lamp lays down a wide circle of pale light on the parking lot, but I can't see anybody.

I hear it again. It's not coming from outside. It's coming from the bedroom.

I open the bedroom door. Michael is standing in the corner in his underpants, crying with his thumb in his mouth.

"Did you wet the bed?" I whisper.

"No." He starts to gulp. When Michael cries a lot, he can't breathe through his nose, and then if he's sucking his thumb, he can't breathe through his mouth, either, and he starts gulping for air.

"Come out here so we don't wake up Mom. What's wrong?"

He stumbles into the living room and sits down in the middle of the floor without taking his thumb out of his mouth.

Just enough light is spilling in from the street-lamp so that I can see his face. It's like all the sadness of the whole world is concentrated there. Two wet tracks of tears stream from his eyes.

"Police are coming for me," he says around his thumb.

"Were you dreaming that?"

He shakes his head.

"Take your thumb out of your mouth and tell me why you think they're coming for you."

"'Cause I stole."

"What'd you steal?"

He won't look at me.

"It's okay. Tell me."

He scrunches his eyes shut and mumbles something and I have to ask him to say it again. "Your mushroom thing," he says.

"My notebook?"

He nods.

"You took my notebook?"

He nods and starts crying again.

"When?"

"Before school."

"Why?"

"Because I'm mad at you."

"Why are you mad at me?"

"Because you won't listen." He starts gulping again.

"Where'd you put it, Michael?"

"You're gonna hate me," he gulps.

"Just tell me."

"Promise you won't hate me."

"You have to tell me."

He wipes snot away with the back of his hand. "I threw it out."

My stomach drops. "Where?"

He points to the kitchen.

I look in the garbage can. There's an almost empty plastic grocery bag in the can; just the macaroni and cheese stuff from dinner is in there.

"Did Mom bring the trash down to the Dumpster today?"

He walks over and stands in the corner like he's giving himself a time-out.

Neither of us says anything for a little while. I'm picturing my notebook in the bottom of a filthy bag in the bottom of a filthy Dumpster.

"You can make another one, can't you, Trev?"

"No."

He starts gulping again.

I put on my shoes.

"Where you going?"

"I'm going to look for it."

"Out there?"

"Where do you think, Michael?"

"Momma's gonna be mad."

"Don't tell her, Michael. You already caused enough problems. Don't wake her up."

I slip out the door.

The hallway is easy. As soon as I get to the stairwell, it gets spookier because you can't see if anybody's waiting below.

I don't want to make any noise, so I try to run lightly. My heart is pounding. The main door rattles when I open it. Broken glass crunches under my feet as I walk down the outside steps. Then I freeze. Something is skittering by the fence. Lightning flashes and a rat scampers through the spotlight of the streetlamp and then disappears in the no-man's-land behind the two buildings. Thunder follows this time.

I run over to the Dumpster. It's a top-loader, big enough to hide a grown-up dead body. Hairs on the back of my neck stand up.

Most people just lift the lid and toss their trash in, so in order to actually see inside, I have to climb up on the side and lift the lid open. Wish I had some of those blue gloves. I lift the lid and the smell almost makes me throw up. Piles and piles of dark bags and garbage not even in bags, just spilling over everything. It's impossible. Even if I knew which bag it was in, even if I could somehow get the bag out, the notebook would be ruined.

I jump down and stare at the Dumpster. I can't help thinking about Charlie. How come some babies get cardboard boxes and other babies get houses like Langley's? That doesn't seem fair. It seems like everybody should start out the same. A real soft blanket and a little bed and some milk. But you can't pick how you start, can you? So, is it luck? Good luck if you end up in Langley's house and bad luck if you end up in a Dumpster? How can something as important as your life be based on luck? And when you know you're not lucky, how are you supposed to feel?

A car pulls into the parking lot, and the head-lights bounce off the Dumpster.

My heart jumps to my throat. I'm not sure if whoever is in the car sees me.

Two big guys get out, their cigarettes glowing red. Maybe they're okay, but you can't trust any-body in a place like Deadly Gardens in the middle of the night. Better to stay still and wait until they're gone.

The front door of our building opens and Michael appears in the doorway. What is he doing down here?

The guys are just beyond our building, so they don't see him, but if Michael calls out to me . . .

Please stay quiet, Michael! Don't say anything.

They keep walking past me, headed for the far building.

Please stay quiet, Michael! Don't say anything.

Michael sees them and he doesn't move. As softly as I can, I run from the Dumpster to our building, looking at Michael with my finger on my lips. *Please stay quiet, Michael! Don't say anything.*

I make it and pull him into the stairwell. "Michael! You shouldn't be down here." I grab him by the arm and pull him up the stairs.

"I wanted to help you find it."

"Help get us killed is more like it."

When we make it inside, I lock our door and lean against it.

"You hate me." He comes rushing at me and buries his face in my stomach.

I don't know who to feel more sorry for . . . him or me. His whole body is shaking.

"You hurted me." He rubs his arm.

"Oh. I hurt you? Don't get me start—" I stop. A picture of Mudman grabbing Diamond by the arm flashes through my mind. "I'm sorry, Michael. Come on, you're like a snot machine. You're getting snot all over me." I peel him off me and get a roll of toilet paper and help him blow his nose. I sit him down at the kitchen table.

He sniffs. "Everybody says I'm garbage and it's true."

"It's not true."

"My backpack is garbage."

"Is this all because you don't have a superhero backpack?"

He nods.

"Some kids are teasing you about that?"

He nods again.

"Man, that makes me want to march in and kick some kindergarten butt."

He laughs one of those just-to-keep-from-crying laughs.

I give him some more toilet paper. "You know what Mom always says."

"What?"

"When people put you down, rise above it. Don't believe the stuff they say about you."

"They say I'm a baby because babies don't have superhero backpacks, either. You say I'm a baby, too." The look he gives me stabs me right through the heart. He's sitting there with his big brown eyes full of tears and his little tummy is going in and out because he's trying so hard to breathe. I remember kindergarten. I remember getting teased about being short and I tried to crawl under Mrs. Kemper's big blue rug. She dragged me out and told me to stop acting like a worm, which made it worse because then I just felt like a short worm.

"Aw, Michael. I don't think you're a baby. You walked all the way down the stairs to come and help me. A baby wouldn't do that. Only time I've called you a baby is when you suck your thumb and I've only been telling you not to do that because I'm worried you'll get teased."

"I don't suck my thumb at school."

"You don't?"

He shakes his head. "They'd really call me a baby if I did."

"Well, see. That's so good, Michael. That's a grown-up way of thinking."

I make him blow his nose again.

"But sometimes when nobody's looking I go in my cubby like this." He pretends he's sticking his head in his cubby and he takes a quick suck on his thumb and then he pops it out.

I have to laugh because he looks like a tiny cigarette addict taking a puff.

"You're laughing at me."

"No, man. I think that's real smooth. It's like your secret way of taking care of yourself. It's like you know what you need."

"I know what I need. I need a new backpack." He lays the words down again like a bricklayer.

Something catches in my throat. It kills me to imagine him waking up every morning and dreading what everybody's going to be saying about him. "Hey, Michael," I say.

"What?"

"I've got an idea." I bring his backpack and my markers over to the window where I can see better. "I'll draw a superhero on your backpack. Who do you want? Spider-Man? Superman? The Hulk?

No, don't pick that. I don't have a good green."

"You gonna draw one?"

"Yeah."

"It won't look store-bought. Those kind are puffy."

"I know what you mean. But I'm going to do something new. I'm going to make up a special brand-new graffiti-style, supercool superhero that nobody else has, so nobody can compare it to anything. You just say it's your own superhero."

"What power does he have?"

"What power do you want?"

"Crime-fighting power."

"You got it. See, this boy looks like an ordinary boy, but he's got crime-fighting power in his . . . thumb! When he sees a crime, he secretly sucks his thumb and becomes . . . Thumbman!"

Michael's eyes light up.

He tells me exactly how he wants it to look.

"You like it?"

Michael nods.

"Is it cool?"

"It's cool."

"So here's what you do. You wear your back-pack and if anybody tells you you're garbage, just hold your thumb and look at them like this. . . ." I stare at him without blinking.

"What does that do?" Michael asks.

"It makes you powerful. Whenever Thumbman stares at anybody, they can see the power in his eyes and they know he's a superhero and they back off. Go ahead and try it."

Michael leans in and makes his eyes big and stares at me.

His eyes are all Michael. It's like the whole

of his soul is in there and he's trying so hard to succeed and be powerful even though he's just a little guy, and it makes tears jump into my eyes. But that's not what he's going for at all, so I blink back my tears and I say, "Whoa!" And I fall off my chair. "That was powerful."

Mom walks in, still half asleep. "What is this? A midnight tea party?"

"I'm a superhero," Michael says. "Tomorrow when I go to school I'm gonna show everybody."

Mom is totally confused.

I try to explain about the notebook and she starts having a fit when I get to the part about how I went to look for it. After I calm her down she has to lecture us. I guess when you're a mom it's never too late for a lecture.

"Michael, you shouldn't have thrown that note-book away. Did you say sorry? If you do something you know is wrong, you have to say sorry or bad feelings will just eat away at you."

"Sorry," Michael says.

"Now about that notebook," she says, and a magic trick unfolds before our eyes. She walks over to the refrigerator and reaches for something next to her orange shoe box. It's my notebook. "Ta-da!" she says, and hands it to me. "I saw it in the trash and thought it looked important. Tish wanted to get at it, so I put it up high, and with all the commotion I forgot to tell you about it."

I can't believe it.

"Is it okay?" Michael asks.

"It's okay."

Michael cracks my heart wide open with his smile.

36.
MOM

Mom puts Michael to bed. I sit down on my mattress and look out the window. The lightning has stopped and it still hasn't rained.

After a minute, Mom comes over. "Trev, that thing with the backpack? You're a genius. He's actually excited to go to school." She walks over and slides down, back against the wall, until she's sitting next to me. "We should both be asleep right now. How come we're awake?"

I shrug.

She stretches her legs out. Her toes are skinny. Mine, too.

"Holy mackerel," she says. "Your legs are almost as long as mine."

We sit quietly. Somewhere in the far, far distance a siren moans. Somebody somewhere is hurt or sick. Or maybe it's a false alarm. That would be nice.

She taps the side of my foot with hers. "I told Michael to say sorry, but I don't think I did. I'm sorry I jumped to conclusions about you doing graffiti and stealing."

"Do you really believe me?"

She nods. "But from my point of view you have to admit things weren't looking too good. You got a detention for being late, you got two detentions for causing trouble on the bus. I told you no travel team soccer and you went behind my back and tried out anyway. A cop brings you home and then you go out in the middle of the night and practically get yourself killed. I swear, Trev. Any more excitement and I'm gonna have me a complete heart attack. Youngest woman to ever die of a complete heart attack."

"Things were going good at first. But Diamond

kept getting in my face, and then this whole war with Xander got started. I don't have proof that he's framed me, but he is a parasitic fungus."

She laughs. "That's a new one."

"See, I learned that from Mr. Ferguson, but I won't be able to be in his class anymore, because everybody thinks I'm just one of the dregs."

"They do not."

"'The people from those apartments are the dregs'—Xander's dad said that to Mr. Gonzalez."

My mom's face turns red.

"You have to rise above it, Trev. Xander's dad has no idea—"

A statement comes out of me like one of those big black anvils that come out of the sky in cartoons. I say, "At least he has a dad."

My mom looks at me, surprised, because we have this unspoken agreement not to really talk about him.

"There's nothing I can do about that," she says. "I know the dad thing is hard, but I don't want you to be ashamed of anything. What your dad did was your dad's problem. You're not him. Okay?"

She nudges me with her foot. "Okay?"

"Is there . . . any chance he was innocent?"

I see the answer in her face.

"Wait, Trev." She looks at me and there's something new in her eyes. She gets up and takes the orange shoe box down from the refrigerator and tugs off the rubber band. She lifts out our stack of photos and pulls out some envelopes from the bottom. From one of them she takes out a photograph and hands it to me. I hold it toward the light coming in from the window so I can see it.

My throat closes up. I've never seen this picture.

"He was seventeen when I took that."

There's this guy with this huge smile, mugging for the camera.

"He looks like me," I say.

She nods. "I was always worried that you would see yourself in him and—I don't know—take it on or feel ashamed. And I never wanted you to feel ashamed because none of that was your fault, so I figured I just wouldn't talk about him. But I know it kills you to have a dad in jail. I know that."

I don't think I'm even breathing.

She goes on. "He had some good qualities and the truth is you got those, Trev. He was funny. So are you. He could always make me laugh. He's artistic. I never told you that. He could draw, but he never did anything with it. You got your good looks from him, too."

"Was he mean—is he mean?"

She shakes her head. "He got mixed up with drugs and then started stealing to buy them. He was never mean, just messed up."

"Is he . . . do you ever talk to him?"

"I brought you with me when I visited him in the beginning. You were too little to remember. He would always light up when he saw you. But then I got worried because I didn't want you to get attached to him. I didn't want you to think you had some daddy who was going to get out and come back and make everything okay. And I had to move on, too. The truth is that he is messed up, Trev. He was a good person. He really was. But he was so young and he got messed up with drugs and it ruined him. Maybe he'll change. I don't know. Maybe when you're older you can meet him and make up your own mind about him, but right now it's just us. It's just you and me and Michael and Tish. I'm sorry."

She stares at the hole in the wall, trying not to cry. "I feel terrible about the soccer thing, Trev. But I can't say yes, even though I know how much you want to play. Even if we could afford it, there's no way I could get you to all those games and practices." Her eyes are filled to the brim. "There's lots of things you want, and you're mad at me because I'm not the kind of mom you wish you had. I don't have a high school diploma. I don't have a decent job. I don't have a car or a nice apartment. I can't give you anything you want. I'm so sorry, Trevor." Her voice chokes up. "I'm not a very good mom."

Now I'm the one turning into a statue.

She sniffs and blinks and a few tears come out. "I'm going to tell you the truth, Trevor. Sometimes I get so tired and I just want to lay down and die. I'm trying so hard, but I don't know how to get out of this hole. The minute I make a little money, it's gone." The tears start rolling down. "And then you make a superhero for Michael . . ." She smiles, even though she's crying. "And all this love just fills me up. And I feel so lucky." She shakes her head and smiles again.

I can't look at her because if I do I'll start crying.

"Look. . . ." She goes through the photos until she finds the one she wants and then she hands it to me. I know this one. It's from the hospital. I was just born and my mom is holding me in her arms. In the picture she is looking down at me and smiling and she looks happy and really scared at the same time.

"You look like you're holding a bomb in your arms," I say.

She laughs and wipes her eyes with the back of her hand. "I was scared. But it was like a bomb of something good. Like flowers or something. Look at you. You were this tiny thing and I had to figure out how to take care of you."

My face is all scrunched and wise-looking and my eyes are closed. I am wrapped up snug in a soft blue blanket, like Charlie should have had.

"Okay, I'm gonna tell you something weird." She sits back down and scoots in closer so we can both look at the picture. "When you were inside me, I swear I could hear your thoughts. Not thoughts. I mean, you didn't know how to talk, so it wasn't thoughts in words. It was more like thoughts in feelings. And I swear you could feel my thoughts. I'd talk to you all the time. Not out loud. I'd just think things to you, like 'Hey, baby, don't worry. Everything's gonna be all right.'"

She laughs. "And then after you were born, I still felt that connection. You could be in the next room crying, let's say because you were scared because I went to get something and you couldn't see me, and I could just think my thoughts to you. 'It's okay, baby, Momma's right here.' And if I was doing it right . . . really concentrating . . . you'd feel those thoughts and you'd stop crying." She smiles at me. "And you know what? I still do it. I think it's harder now because there are so many more noises. But sometimes when you're at school or whatever, I send a thought to you." She closes her eyes. *"Hey, Trevor. Rise above it."* She wiggles her fingers at me like she's sending me a message on an invisible line through the air.

I jolt like the message just zapped into my brain and we both laugh.

"Is it crazy?" she asks.

I shake my head.

She takes my face in her hands and looks into my eyes. "You broke my heart when you said I probably wished I had thrown you in a Dumpster. Don't ever say that again. You keep me going. Don't you know that?"

She pulls me in for a hug and I can't help it anymore. I start to cry.

She gets the same toilet paper roll Michael was using and gives us each a piece. We blow our noses. "I'm working in the Fry Factory and living in the Cry Factory," she says, which makes me laugh.

"Good one, Mom."

She laughs and blows her nose.

I blow my nose.

"You sound like a goose," she says.

"You, too."

We blow our noses at the same time and crack up.

"Mom—"

She looks up.

"You know when I said I wished I was born to someone else?"

Her eyes fill up again.

"I didn't mean it," I say.

That makes her start to cry again. "Yeah, you did."

"No, I didn't."

"Yeah, you did."

"Shut up. I didn't."

"Did you just tell me to shut up?"

"What I mean is you're the only mom I've got."

She laughs through her tears. "Better than nothing, huh?"

"No. I mean . . ." How can I explain what I mean? I look at the photo. I'm in a blanket and my mom is holding me and she's smiling, and I can almost see all the invisible lines that run from her to me. Even though she's scared, she's sending good thoughts my way and promising to take care of me and even after I was born she kept holding me and sending good thoughts my way and feeding me and worrying about me and making sure I didn't put broken glass in my mouth and yelling at me when I did something wrong so I wouldn't do it again. And if I was crying and thinking something like *Help! I need water!* she was listening and saying, "Here's some water, baby. Everything's going to be all right."

I look up. Her face is a mess and her hair is half pulled in a ponytail and half falling down. "What I mean . . . you know how you said that it's just you and me and Michael and Tish?"

"Yeah."

I think about Michael's worried Little Man face and Tish's fierce Little Cavewoman face. "It's okay if it's just us. Us is good."

She smiles at me through her tears.

"Us is good." She kisses me and sniffs.

My stomach growls and she laughs.

"You didn't eat, did you?" She wipes her face with the palm of her hand. "Enough of this crying. Let's have a midnight snack. I'm hungry, too."

We make peanut butter sandwiches.

"You remember the shelter?" she says between bites.

I nod. I remember sleeping on a cot next to my mom, and I remember being scared and she reached across and held my hand and we fell asleep holding hands.

"I don't want us to ever have to go back there," she says. "That's my goal right now, Trev."

"Well, there was one advantage to that place," I say. "It came with free mushrooms."

She laughs, and then she puts her head down on her arms. "What a night. I'm so tired. I could fall asleep right here."

"Hey, Mom," I say.

"I'm afraid to say what."

"Can we adopt that baby that was found in the Dumpster?"

She lifts her head. "Trevor Musgrove. You knock me out."

"Can we?"

She laughs. "Another baby. That would be something."

"Don't say no."

She groans. "Oh, my bighearted boy. Turn off that brain of yours and go to sleep. Tomorrow is a big day."

We say good night and I curl up on the mattress facing the window.

I look out at the sky. Maybe my dad is out there, thinking about how he messed up his life. Maybe he's missing me. Maybe he's not. I'm not going to let it drag me down. I imagine writing his name on a balloon and opening the window and letting it go. He's out there, but I'm not tied to him anymore.

I get up. There's still a stub of blue chalk left in the windowsill.

Our names are still there. I rewrite them. Make 'em fresh. MOM. MICHAEL. TISH. TREVOR.

CHARLIE, too.

I close my eyes and send a thought his way. *Hang in there, Charlie. I'm thinking about you. I hope you can feel it.*

The sky opens up and it finally starts to rain.

37.
THE MEETING

Ideas probably don't just pop up out of nowhere. They probably have roots, like mycelia, that connect one thought to another to another until an idea pops out like a mushroom. I wake up with one. It may work and it may not. But it's worth a try.

I get my backpack and markers.

Michael comes in, sleepy-eyed. "What are you doing?"

"I'm drawing on my backpack. Don't bump the table, okay? I've got to get this just perfect."

"Is it gonna be a superhero?"

"A superhero would be cool, but I need a logo. Just a little logo right here. You ready for school, Little Man? Let's see your power stare."

Michael leans in and stares like a pint-size Terminator.

I laugh. "You got it!"

Mom hustles in with Tish and Rex.

She reminds me about the meeting and explains that she can't leave until Michael's bus picks him up, but as soon as she can, she'll catch the Ride-On with Tish and Rex. "If I'm late . . . well, I can only do what I can do."

She tells me I should play for the school team. "That's doable," she says. "And then you can make a billion touchdowns and blow those rich guys out of the water."

"That's a really nice thought, Mom. But you don't make touchdowns in soccer. You make goals."

She laughs. "I knew that."

• • •

Outside, the air smells clean. There's a cool little breeze dancing around. Maybe it's carrying some microscopic mushroom spores looking for a nice place to land. Just picturing that helps put me in the right mood.

By the time I walk into the conference room, Xander and both his parents are already there. They are talking with Mr. Gonzalez about some problem with the traffic light in front of the school. "I'll bring my camera and document it!" Mr. Pierce laughs. "That should take care of it."

They stop when I walk in.

I explain that my mom is coming as soon as she can.

Xander's dad doesn't say anything. He just smiles. Then he turns to Mr. Gonzalez. "And what about this girl who was supposedly involved?" His voice is nice and calm, but you can just feel the pod rot creeping out of this guy's smile in all directions.

I don't know what Mr. Gonzalez knows about Diamond, but as he explains that "circumstances of a personal nature are preventing Diamond and her mother from attending," something in his eyes tells me that he knows a lot and that maybe he sees through Mr. Pierce's smile. Maybe the Pierces are even getting under his skin.

I want to scream at Xander's parents that they don't have a clue, and I want to split Xander wide open and show the whole world what he did. But I know that getting all heated up will make the situation worse. If you turn bad to get the bad guy, then the bad guy ends up winning anyway. My mom is right. When you're dealing with people like this, you have to rise above it.

"Diamond didn't do it." I keep my voice as calm as Mr. Pierce's. "I made a mistake about that." Everybody looks at me like I'm going to confess. "And I didn't do it, either. Actually—"

"Please," Xander's father says to Mr. Gonzalez. Now he's getting a little huffy. "Let's not waste time here. We have the proof after all."

"It was in his backpack," Mrs. Pierce adds.

I give Xander my most powerful stare. *I know you did it,* I say with my eyes. I have no proof, but I can see in his eyes that it's true. He shifts. I think he's realizing he might have crossed the line this time.

Mr. Gonzalez clears his throat and smiles back

at the Pierces. "The purpose of the meeting is to hear both sides of the story. Trevor, if you didn't do it, how did the phone get in your backpack?"

Now it's my turn to smile. "I think it was an accident."

"Accident?" Mrs. Pierce barks.

"Our backpacks are both red. Both Nike. I think Xander probably put his phone in my backpack by accident."

Xander looks at me, surprised. He wasn't expecting this.

I set my backpack on the table with my new Nike logo on it. Xander's looks cleaner than mine, but they do look alike.

Xander's dad starts in again, saying that Xander would know which backpack was his.

Then Mr. Gonzalez says, "Let's hear from Xander. Is it possible that you may have made a mistake?"

All eyes on Xander.

He looks at the logo I drew on my backpack. He knows the logo isn't real. He knows I'm giving him a way out, but I don't know if he's going to take it. It's like one of those game shows where a million bucks is resting on the answer to the final question and a big clock is ticking. He's weighing his options. Maybe he's picturing them in his head. What if he fries me for this, and word gets out? What if I tell my side of the story and people like Langley believe me? It's one thing for Xander to put me down when nobody is looking, but to deliberately frame me and get Mommy and Daddy to back him up . . . that can't make him look like anybody's hero. The clock ticks. His face is red. *Come on, Xander. I'm giving you a lifeline. This is your chance to evolve. Take it.*

"It's possible," he finally says.

I wish I had a camera with a zoom lens because Xander's dad looks like he swallowed a toad.

Mr. Gonzalez talks for a while about why this is one of the reasons they don't like kids to have cell phones in school—blah blah blah—and I'm not really listening because my brain is full of the sounds of cheering and the image of confetti falling down from the ceiling.

Then there's nothing more to talk about, and he dismisses Xander and me for class.

Just as we're leaving, Mom walks in. She's got

Tish by the hand and Rex in her arms. She's out of breath. I can tell she ran all the way from the bus stop. Rex is crying, and she's bouncing him to try and make him happy. "I'm sorry I'm late. I got here as fast as I could," she says. She looks like she'd rather jump into a tank with sharks than be here, but she's here.

Mr. Pierce gives my mom a look as they walk out, and I want to kick him right in the butt.

Rise above it.

Mr. Gonzalez explains the "accident" to my mom. He turns out to be not such a bad guy. My mom works up the courage to ask a bunch of questions about how she can help me do better in school.

On the way out, she hoists Rex higher on one hip and asks Mr. Gonzalez if he knows which bus will take her over to Eighth Street.

He tells her and then says, "I appreciate the effort it took you to come in this morning, Ms. Musgrove. I know it isn't easy."

My mom smiles.

38.
RESULTS

On Friday, I head to Mr. Ferguson's room to drop off my Identification Notebook and application for Summit Science and Art. Based on the fact that my notebook is just a sad-looking thing with a cardboard cover, I know I shouldn't expect him to be impressed.

"Ah, Mr. Musgrove," he says when I poke my head in the door. He's wearing a chef hat and an apron and he's cooking something that smells delicious in a frying pan over a burner. "Guess what I'm sautéing in garlic and olive oil?"

"Mushrooms?"

He salutes me with his spatula. "Every year, I am surprised how many students have never tried mushrooms or say they do not like them when they have only eaten button mushrooms in salads."

His first-period students are trickling in. "If we don't want to try one, will we get a bad grade?" one of his students asks.

"Live life large!" he says. "Your taste buds will thank you."

He dishes me up a mushroom on a paper towel. "High in protein. Low in fat," he says. "They contain amino acids, antioxidants, B vitamins, fiber, selenium, and potassium. . . ."

It's warm and juicy and meatier than I imagined.

"What do you think?"

"Surprisingly delicious," I say.

He shrugs as if to say he knew it all along. "As for this"—he points to my notebook and application with his spatula—"I'll get back to you as soon as we have the chance to review it."

I know they're not going to let me in unless they

think I'm worthy. I just really hope I'm worthy.

I hustle to Computer Applications.

"Did you see it?" Juan asks.

"See what?"

"Stevins posted the team list." He grins. "I'm on it!"

"What about me?" I whisper.

"You and Javier and Langley and me. All on the team."

"Xander?"

"Didn't make it." Juan grins and shrugs.

Well, well, well. Looks like Coach Stevins wasn't snowed by Xander. Never underestimate a refrigerator.

Langley catches me in between classes. He says that Xander is telling everybody that the only reason his name isn't on the team roster is because his dad told Stevins he couldn't be on the team. "He told me I should quit, but I said no way back. We're part of the sewer system, right?" He grins and does the official Toilet Swish and a bunch of girls follow him down the hall.

Javier finds out and when I see him later he tells me that he asked Coach Stevins if Xander quit or if he wasn't picked to be on in the first place.

"I don't discuss my decisions with people," the refrigerator said. "I will only say that I choose people who I think will be good team players."

Javier laughs when he tells me this because he thinks it's Stevins's way of saying that Xander wasn't chosen. "Everybody knows Xander isn't a good team player," he says.

I don't know if it's true, and I don't care. I'm not going to worry about Xander Pierce anymore. It just feels good to know I'm on a team. Even if it is the Toilets.

During lunch and P.E., Xander tells everybody at least twelve times that his dad made Stevins take his name off the roster. I just listen and smile. *Whatever, Xander. Whatever.*

On my way out, I pass by the music room and a big poster board sign catches my eye.

AUDITION RESULTS
CONGRATULATIONS TO EVERYONE WHO AUDITIONED!
IT WAS THE BIGGEST TURNOUT EVER.
UNFORTUNATELY, WE HAVE TO LIMIT
THE NUMBER OF ACTS.
FOR THOSE OF YOU WHO DIDN'T MAKE IT,
PLEASE FEEL FREE TO COME TO ME FOR COMMENTS.
THE NEW "STARS" OF THIS YEAR'S
STARS SHOW WILL BE:
1. DIAMOND FOLLET
2. TRACY MILLBURN
3. KEISHA SAMUELS

As soon as I see it I know what I want to do.

39.
BREAKING THROUGH

When I get home from school, I run straight to Diamond's apartment building. I hesitate at the front door thinking, *What if they let Mudman loose?* but I push myself inside. I run up to her floor and knock. No one answers.

I want to try Saint Francis, which is the closest hospital to us. Mom says it's a long shot. She is guessing social services moved Diamond and her mom to a special shelter just for women.

"If I go to the hospital and she's still there, will they let me see her?"

"Maybe," Mom says. "If she's still there. You

have to go to the front desk and explain you're a friend."

"Why do you want to go to the hospital?" Michael asks.

"I want to tell Diamond something."

"That singing girl?"

"Yep."

"What do you want to tell her?"

"Just something."

It's not far, so I decide to run—get me in shape for the season. I promise I'll be back in time because the Fry Factory is giving Mom another chance and letting her start at five thirty instead of five o'clock.

"They must be nice," Michael says.

"They must be desperate," Mom says.

The hospital is huge and it's hard to figure out which door to go in. Finally I get to a wide, curved, silver desk with three computers, and sitting behind it, there's a wide, curvy woman with lots of hair piled on top of her head. I figure she's going to be all official and cold, like the desk, but when I ask if Diamond Follet is there and can I visit her because I'm a friend, a smile pops out. "Isn't that sweet," she says, and taps Diamond's name into the computer with rainbow fingernails, flashy enough to compete with Ms. Beitz's. "Sorry, honey. Checked out."

"Is there a way you can tell me where she went, like another hospital or shelter?" I ask.

She apologizes and says she can't and calls out, "Good luck," to me.

As I'm leaving, I notice a tucked-in spot where there's a statue of a saint. On the floor all around it are teddy bears and rattles and a bunch of cards and a sign that says, TO MAKE A DONATION, PLEASE SEE THE FRONT DESK. Taped to the sign, there's a photograph of a baby wrapped in a blanket, and there's a doctor or a nurse's hand in the picture, and the baby is holding on to the person's index finger. His eyes are closed and he has a tube up his nose.

It's Charlie. I know it.

"He's here? That baby from the Dumpster?" I ask the woman.

She nods, her mouth full because she just took

a bite of a muffin. After she swallows and wipes the crumbs off, she says, "Everybody's rooting for him. People keep bringing him little presents and saying prayers and donating money."

"Is he going to be okay? Can I see him?"

She smiles. "No visitors allowed, but come around here and I'll show you something."

As I walk around the desk, she scoots her chair over to one of the other computers and taps something in. She moves the screen so I can see. "We call it Babycam. One of the nurses set it up because we kept asking how he was doing. He was in bad shape, but he's not a preemie, so once the antibiotics kicked in, he started improving fast. Look at him."

On the screen is a video of Charlie. He's sleeping in a little white T-shirt and he has kicked his blanket down so you can see his soft tummy going in and out, slow and steady.

She smiles. "That's him right now. This is live."

His hands are in fists covering up his face, but then he moves and stretches one hand out, opening up fingers and closing them again in a kind of slow motion. No more tubes up his nose. His eyelids are smooth. He looks like he's having a nice little dream.

She taps the screen with one of her rainbow fingernails. "Hey, sweetie! Hey, sweetie, we're watching you," she says.

I look at him and imagine my thoughts going right through the computer and into his mind. *Hey, Charlie, hang in there. Everybody's rooting for you. Everything's going to be all right.*

He stretches again, and his tiny mouth opens in a perfectly oval yawn, and we both laugh.

I'm coming back another day to check on you, Charlie. So don't go getting in any trouble. His face settles down and his tummy goes in and out again, slow and steady and soft.

On the run back home, my feet don't even hurt. My blisters must have healed.

● ● ●

I'm running toward our building when Michael calls down from our window. "She's there, Trev!"

He points to the Ride-On stop at the far end of our street. "The singing girl was here and now she's leaving!"

I run. Diamond is at the bus stop following a woman onto the bus with a garbage bag in her good arm.

I shift into high gear. "Wait—"

The bus takes off.

"Wait—"

My feet barely touch the ground. The bus stops and I give it everything I've got. The door opens, and I climb on, breathless.

"You're lucky I'm in a good mood," the bus driver says as I flash my school ID.

The minute the doors close, I realize that I have no idea what I'm going to say. Too late to go back now.

Diamond is looking at me, surprised, the left side of her face still bruised and swollen. With one hand, she's wiping away tears. The other arm is in a bright pink cast. She's sitting with a woman in the last seat on the left side of the bus, her big garbage bag blocking the aisle next to her.

The seat next to her on the right is open. I step over her garbage bag and sit down next to a big old grandpa of a guy who's got his eyes closed.

"Fancy meeting you here," she says. "Where you headed?"

"I'm . . . I'm going to a friend's," I say.

"Where?"

I don't know how to answer since I don't even know which bus I've just gotten on, so I finesse a change of subject. "Hey, did anybody tell you?"

"Tell me what?"

"You made it."

"What are you talking about?"

"The Stars Show. You made it."

"I did?" She breaks into a smile. "I made the school talent show," she says to the woman next to her.

"That's nice," the woman says.

The bus rumbles over a pothole.

I don't know for sure what Diamond is thinking, but she's quiet.

"Where are you going?" I ask.

"Bus station. This is my aunt. We're going to live with her for a while."

Her aunt has on big glasses and her mouth is closed up like a clam.

"My mom is coming later." Diamond sees my face and adds, "She's okay."

"Will you still be at school?" I ask.

Diamond's aunt gives her a look like don't go blabbing all the details.

Diamond shifts her position and looks out the back window. "Nah. Different school." She's sad and she doesn't want me to see it. She must be like my mom. She doesn't like anybody seeing her cry.

"Maybe you can come back and be in the show," I say.

She shrugs. "Who cares."

The bus pulls over. The grandpa beside me wants to get off, so I have to climb over the garbage bag, and then hold it up so he can get out.

Her aunt leans against the window and closes her eyes.

"That baby is going to be okay," I say. "That Dumpster baby."

"You finally get a TV?" she asks.

I have to smile because I did kind of see him on TV. It seems too complicated to explain about the hospital and the Babycam, so I just laugh it off.

"That's good that he's okay," she says.

The bus rumbles over another pothole, and a confession pops out of me.

"You know, I made up a nickname for you," I say.

"What?"

"Microphone Mouth."

She laughs.

After a few seconds, I just say it. "I'm sorry I told Mr. Gonzalez that you put the cell phone in my backpack."

She looks at me. And then she shrugs. "I can see why you did—because of the pen and everything, I mean. I was thinking about that just this morning."

I nod. Done.

The bus turns a corner. It's a street I've never been on.

I should get off, but it doesn't feel complete. I wish I had something to give her for good luck.

"Hey, you got a marker?" I ask.

"Bottom pocket." She turns so her backpack is facing me, and I unzip the bottom pocket. Inside is the silver marker that she took back right before Mudman came. I face the aisle and put one leg up so she can rest her cast on my knee. Then I start to draw. It's a real high-quality pen. Permanent ink. Comes out looking just like liquid silver. I can only draw when the bus is at a stop sign, so it takes me a few stops to get it done.

She goes crazy over it.

Looks good, even if I do say so myself.

The bus pulls over.

I give her back the pen and get up to go and we catch eyes.

She was the first person I met at Deadly Gardens, the one who told us what was going on with Charlie. I guess you never know how your life is going to connect with other people's lives.

"See you later, Mushroom," she says, and grins.

"See you later, Microphone Mouth." I walk up the aisle. The door whooshes open.

"Hey," I call back. "I'll buy your song when it comes out."

Her smile lights up the whole bus. She tilts her head back and lets it rip, *"Baby, if you love me, set me free!"*

As I get off, I hear people clapping. She leans over her aunt and calls out the window, "Who's your friend who lives here?"

"What's it to you?" I ask.

"Just wondering." She smiles and tosses me the silver pen, and the bus pulls away.

I only have to wait a few minutes for a bus back, which means no problem getting home in time for Mom to go to work, and I don't know if it's just me but everybody seems like they get on in a good mood today. I look at each person and try to guess where they're going and what they're going to do. When I get to the Deadly Gardens stop, there's Juan at the far end of the parking lot, juggling. Maybe I can bring Michael and Tish down and we can all pass the ball around. It's time the little guys learned some soccer skills.

I pass by the Deadly Gardens sign and stop. The ground around it is muddy and littered with dead leaves, broken glass, cigarette butts, and a half-buried candy wrapper. But there, right next to one of the signposts, is a beautiful brown mushroom sticking up on a perfectly straight long stem, as clean as can be.

Caramel-colored wavy cap. Dark brown gills. Silky stem. Cap open like an umbrella.

I swear there was nothing here yesterday but trash.

I crouch down. Miles of mycelia must be under

this ground right here, under my feet, growing and making all these invisible connections and producing this perfect little guy. Miles of mycelia under my feet right at this moment.

Juan sees me. He's jogging over. It's crazy. He's going to ask me what I'm looking at that's so interesting.

I'm going to say, "A mushroom."

402-HOST

HELP WANTED

Day-care provider
needed 9-4.
May bring own
child. For more
information
please call
6120122

Art Assignment

from Mr. Raye

HOW TO MAKE YOUR OWN RUBBER STAMP

① ERASER

② ERASER

carve the eraser

TiPS for: MUSHROOM HUNTiNG

- Go after it rains.
- Find out which kind of mushrooms are "in season" for your area so you know what to look for. Certain mushrooms appear around or on certain trees.
- Look around the base of live trees and on dead trees and stumps. Look under dead leaves, especially if a spot of leaf litter looks like something is lifting it slightly from underneath.

~ GOOD LUCK! ~

Acknowledgments

A mycelial-like network of people supported my efforts in the writing of this book. Corinna Thornton, Jan Shauer, and Frances Evangelista all said yes when I asked them to read the earliest draft, and their comments were insightful. An interview in a great magazine—*The Sun*—introduced me to the work of Paul Stamets and inspired me to read his book *Mycelium Running: How Mushrooms Can Help Save the World* (Berkeley: Ten Speed Press, 2005). Stamets's book and company, Fungi Perfecti, inspired me to inoculate my story with mycelia, and his comments on the final draft were much appreciated. I was also inspired and informed by the charming picture book *Katya's Book of Mushrooms*, by Katya Arnold and Sam Swope (New York: Henry Holt and Company, 1977); and an excellent pod-rot article on the USDA website's Sci4Kids, "Attack of the Witches'-Broom!" by Hank Becker. The members of the Mycological Association of Washington (D.C.) greeted me warmly and responded enthusiastically to mycological questions, especially Raymond LaSala, Waldemar Poppe, and Reed Richter, the latter of whom also made comments on a draft.

When I was knocked flat by the writing process, Darcy Pattison's *Novel Metamorphosis: Uncommon Ways to Revise* reminded me which bootstraps to use in order to pull myself up again. My admiration and thanks go to Noe Bravo, Manuel Martinez, Carlos Sosa, and Adolfo Lopez. Their fine skill and hard work inspired me to keep working during the hardest times. A fond nod must also go to science teacher Dan Lerner, who taught my kids to "perambulate to the egress."

Heartfelt thanks to my friends: Jim Kuhn and Pete Looney for presenting me with beautiful mushroom photographs; the Leblanc family for providing me with a much-needed writing retreat; Mary Naden for understanding what it means to be on deadline; Karen Giacopuzzi for pitching in to help and for providing key insights on the final manuscript, especially during the crunch time; and Richard Washer for always responding to my calls with the perfect combination of encouragement, humor, compassion, and practical advice. Above all, thanks to my editor, Regina Griffin, for believing in this book even when I wasn't sure I would ever finish; and to my family, Ivan, Max, and Simon, for reading drafts, listening to me vent, and understanding, with such patience and love, my need to disappear into another world from time to time. I'm grateful.

MARY AMATO

is the author of *The Word Eater* and *The Naked Mole-Rat Letters*, two beloved middle-grade novels that have appeared on numerous state lists. While she may be best known for her writing, Mary is also a cofounder of Firefly Shadow Theater (a puppet company now based in Princeton, Massachusetts), a musician in a group called Two-Piece Suit, as well as a teacher of creative writing. She lives in Maryland with her husband, Ivan, a science writer, and her two sons. Visit her online at www.maryamato.com.